3500

RAPAHO

BY JAMIE LEE COOPER

SHADOW OF A STAR

THE HORN AND THE FOREST

RAPAHO

by Jamie Lee Cooper

THE BOBBS-MERRILL COMPANY, INC.
A SUBSIDIARY OF HOWARD W. SAMS & CO., INC.
PUBLISHERS / INDIANAPOLIS · KANSAS CITY · NEW YORK

For three good friends

Robert Amussen
who let me
write this book

Robert Mitchner
who urged me to
write this book

Gertrude L. Ward
who read this book
as I was writing it

RAPAHO

✳ We never say good-bye—it's an old Shawnee custom that we stole. We just pack up our guns and hides, bury our troubles by some pine, and we go out. And leave. And take our footprints with us. And our whistling. And are no more where once we were. So that we are like the dead.

(The boy came home from huntin down on the Tennessee and no one was there. Varmints had torn at the cabin and carried off all likely things, though hunter folks, they don't leave much behind in way of properties cause they ain't got much. Him there standin, and them gone. God knows where. Just couldn't wait for him. Him grown, though, fifteen and tall. They had taken his girl-bride with them and they reckoned he would find them somewhere out there . . . beyond. He was good at trackin and so he started out and went beyond when he hadn't reckoned . . . hadn't planned . . . hadn't thought to go beyond. Had thought to make himself a merchant up at Louisville, but had to go beyond because that's where they were and his girl-bride with her cornhusk doll.)

Some settler man once said (and this was when we left Kaintuck) he meant to stay, to build a cabin where his wagon sat with its tongue lolled in the

1

dirt under the hide thrown over it to make a tent where his young'uns had slept good three nights since straddling the Allegheny Fall. The rest of us who heard it looked at him and stepped away. Stay? *Stay?* STAY? We stepped away from such a crazy man and held our young'uns hard against our legs before they heard that awful word the man had said and asked, What does it mean? And we went out. Out where? Why, to beyond. Just beyond. Out there where it is—that's where beyond. We went out with every tongue sweet as a willow whistle sucking on the Wide Mizzourye for we were bound to rolleree away and across the wide Mizzourye with Preacher Jesse S. to part the waters for us.

Let that man stay. Let him never step foot farther'n Edsell's Store and be buried with his hands folded under the lilac by his sawed-plank door. Not us. Not us. We're never known to stay anyplace longer'n it takes to come up on it, walk in it, and slip on past. Let that man stay while we go with Preacher Jesse S. to meet the Sye-ox and smoke his pipe and do a little huntin on the land that was no El Dorado for the Spaniard and we will whistle the Wide Mizzourye where every thunderbolt is straight from Kingdom Come.

(The hound was runnin with the wolves where he had no business to be, and when he came home, they were gone. Gone off without him, him that saved the baby from the bear that time when it was still a dark and bloody ground. Him with the scars to show around his head, below his ribs, and on one leg. Him that could wind a Shawnee two miles off, if there were any left to wind. But the hound had trotted behind the wagon all the way from Carolina and he reckoned he could trot some more. So he sniffed around the stoop and found their trail and started off, nosin and bayin as he ran though they had two days start on him.)

You could say it was a song. Yes, it was a sort of song. I mean, the way we went. The way that Preacher Jesse S. made us so restless. Yes, it was a song. No common song. Rather like a psalm. Or maybe like a hymn. Hymns are full of going on forever to God knows where, and that's the way that this was—just a going song.

"Let us get ourselves hence and go forth out to the Sye-ox land," the Preacher said, "for it's the Promised Land that we was promised and didn't get."

And Preacher Jesse S. spit it out in rhyme:

> "Listen to me shoutin Promised Land—
>   Promised Land!
> Come to me and take me by the hand—by
>   the hand.
> Hear them crickets callin chicka chay—
>   chicka chay.
> Children, they are sayin—Go away—Go away!

> "Blazes old—Shawnees dead.
> Trails is cold—meat is bread.
> Looky there—a arrowhead!
> Stoneboats creakin—land is broke.
> Axes shriekin—woods is smoke.
> Was a bobcat denned that oak."

> "They ain't no game left on Paint Lick,
> Cumberland, Panther, Eagle Crick.
> Danged settlers has driv it beyond them
>   gaps
> Whackin with their axes like thunderclaps
> Their clumsy plows springin traps.
> Prayin and preachin and plantin by Aries
> Talkin to the Injuns like missionaries

Cuttin the woods up into prairies.
Shootin off their guns just to hear their
     booms
Bringin in traders like their danged heir-
     looms
Turnin the game licks into tombs.
We gotta get gone
While summer hangs on
We gotta go where the game's a waitin
Cause
Hunger's a scarecrow flappin in the snow,
Hunger's a plowed field where tamed crops
     grow,
Hunger's a drunken settlement Injun,
Hunger's the smell of homespun, cinna-
     mon.
The game is thick on the Niobrara,
Cimarron, Platte, Cienega,
Smoky Hill, Peace, Wounded Knee,
Arkansas, Loup, Milk, Pawnee.
West of Kaintuck, beyond Laramie
North and south of the Missouri
From the sand of the Apache to the woods
     of the Cree
The land is every man's and free.
They ain't a tree
A honeybee
Ain't nothin out there but a sea
Of game."

So, like he said, we girded up our loins to go forth
and begone out to the Promised Land. Well, we didn't
want to stay anyway—I told you that. But we hadn't
figured to go so fast so far to beyond.

(The trader come with his wagon piled with calico and salt, shot and guns, powder, seven bonnets—

big investment—and yards of lace—bigger investment—and liquor—best investment. And they were
gone. A panther was standin on the table in their
cabin and yellow-eyed him back. So he just whistled
and shoved his hat back on his head and whipped up
his team and said, Looks like we're a goin on beyond.)

But ain't you never goin to build a home? The settler man again—when he saw us packing up
he asked weren't we ever goin to build a home.
Home? *Home?* HOME? we said. Why don't you know
that you can't build no home—home is where you're
born and taken from. It's where you go away from.
It's what you leave behind—a roof to fall down after
and a fence that only kept the scarecrow in and
nothin out and a graveplot to be covered by the
brambles and a button to be found by some young'un
later on. Long after you are gone. Long after when
some settler man comes to take the old logs from
your place. Looky yere . . . a button, the young'un
says. And then it finds the bit of lace ma bought that
time at Parkersburg, never had a thing fine enough
to sew it on, so threw it down in bitterness when we
packed to go. The bit of lace kept so protected and so
clean between the pages of the Bible all those years
while her young'uns were bein born—only to be
thrown down in the dirt with all the other things too
fine to want. The bit of lace bought for ants
and spiders in the end. Ma didn't need the lace—she
only thought she did, for the silver spiderwebs in all
the vasty forests were ma's true lace and needed no
Bible to protect them. Looky yere . . . a bullet in a
tree, the young'un says and goes on to say, I 'member
that . . . was when their grandpa missed the bear.
And looky yere, the young'un says, an old pot their
ma forgot. No, not forgot, we know, but set back to

5

leave at home because it was her ma's and her ma is dead out there beneath the dogwood. Not forgot, but scrubbed with twigs and wiped with the greasy rag and turned over in the corner to be the last thing she saw shinin in the cabin as her shadow left the door. Home. Poor man. You can't build a home—homes're built by fathers for their sons, not by fathers for their ownselves so you might as well forget it and come along with us. Home. Such a word to use out here in this glorious and wildy land. Poor tetched man. Full of words like *stay* and *home*. Next he'll be sayin *plant* and offer us some wheat. What words! We sighed when we looked back at him axein at a tree to make a home and stay and likely plant.

(The halfbreed outcast came to beg his bread like always, pounded on the door, and they were gone. Gone where? Gone where? he yelled inside in Shawnee like his pa had spoke. But no one answered back. He moved into the cabin what he had—what was on his back plus a knife. But it was lonesome with those graves beyond the door and dried human tracks across the dooryard and no one to give him bread or talk to him in Shawnee. The new men coming in, they didn't understand about the Shawnees, had never even heard of the Kentahkehs who'd heard some going song before and gone off after their own beyond. So he packed up what he had—what was on his back, the knife, a mothy brown bearskin found in the loft, a johnnycake board found in the creek— and he went too, following after them, scratching his head to remember how to read the sign and wishing there was someone to say, This way . . . this way to the beyond where they have gone.)

This song, this going song, we could put in simpler words than Preacher Jesse S. had said. They were our own words, we who can only read the hunted and

6

the hunter's sign and in our shamed unknowingness have to trust the Preacher when he says there is a tribe called Sye-ox and a Promised Land that Moses missed.

We're a goin out beyond.

Those were the words. They Virginia-Reeled across the dark and bloody ground, no longer dark and bloody, but long Stated (like we say) or granted Statehood (like you say) and rightly called Kentucky, though none can tell you what it means.

These words, they took us like a fever and we went out whistling and never looking back.

We took the same things with us that we always took:

The old wagons that had leaned under some hickory tree mossing and rotting since we had ridden them in. The poor old horse or ox that thought this time we'd really stopped. Packets of corn to plant— yes, we plant corn like Injuns, there's no shame in that. Seeds to cure things like we knew such as the ague. The women sewed the corn seeds in bits of calico and let them pile in heaps on the dried-mud floors . . .

The dear dear floor—good as ary I seen back East, though anty come spring and summer, a little crickety, too, but never wormy except so much as my boy gets some to fish with.

The guns and knives and shot and powder and traps and extra pelts to keep a body warm . . .

Lands of milk and honey are likely to be warm, so don't pack much. And the Sye-ox will look after us, just like the Shawnee did.

The axes, adzes, kettles, but no dishes . . .

I reckon we can bury the platter under the floor, though I don't know why . . . likely we won't be back this way again.

We left behind the same things we always left. All else.

And good-bye to our dead sons and daughters, our Siseras and Micahs, and our folks and all other kin. Good-bye inside—not out—because I told you we don't ever say it. The reins flick and other feet set themselves on paths, feet without wagons, they set themselves on paths. The packs are shifted and the rifles slung on shoulders and the hounds whistled to and we are off to go beyond and we are off with a new song in our whistle to take the place of the old songs which went sour. Done with our Yankee Doodle Doodling and our loves we'd given cherries to and our Billy Boys so long at fairs. The nearest our song comes to one you might've heard is that of the Wayfaring Stranger who's going to cross the Jordan in the morning. But it's the wide Mizzourye we were headin for, and not the Jordan, God willing and the baby doesn't sicken nor the horse break a leg and spare the axles splittin and make my feet hold out and don't let strange fevers catch us in the flats.

We went beyond to walk a wilderness. To be strengthened by our own pillar of fire lit by the hired Leavenworth scout who moved a day ahead of us. To finally believe that Preacher Jesse S. really talked to God when he camped away from us up in the hills. To feast on the prairie hen. But when we crossed the wide Mizzourye, no waters parted for us. The nights got hot. The wind burned down the grass. We found ourselves in the open places of beyond and thirsted at the empty waterhole and wiped the horses' and the oxen's tongues with dampened rags from the last black dregs of water from that dark and bloody ground.

'Twas so sweet . . . the water when we left . . . and

now so dark . . . like 'lasses, only bitter and the baby throws it up.

Our whistling faltered when we stood beside the hurried graves scratched out by the sick men who divided the last meal after the woman died in childbirth, the knife beneath her bed of skins not cutting out the pain so that her eyes popped from her head and she cried out her own song of torn-apart by her child who had never heard the song we left behind nor the one we were following after. You know it—the great song of the beyond where we have come. The song of game. The Promised Land.

This is the land that we were promised and that we got.

We had forgotten that we ever whistled when we saw the smoke puff up from shivering hills and wondered silently each one . . . but did not speak . . . too tired to speak . . . but wondered silently each one and tried to hear the words the smoke throbbed out. *White men we can kill.* Is that what it was saying? Or something else. Hopefully. Something else. *Friendly talk, come and eat.* Yes, like the Shawnees used to do in the olden golden olden golden days before the last one fell with a settler's bullet in his head and the pack of pelts he was carrying to trade at Edsell's Store still in his arms.

This is the song of beyond, of the Promised Land where no promises are kept.

We made a stand on an alien dark and bloody ground and we remembered those cabins that fell down as we went out—never looking back—those triumphal arches (that's what the Preacher called them) of the Shawnee wars that we had won. Those wagons we should have just let moss and rot. Those graves with which we paid for what we won. And we

9

remembered the wobbly fence as the Preacher's fiddle got its neck torn off. And we remembered the wolves of our woods as the catgut cried like a coyote. And we remembered Edsell's Store and the bit of lace and the shiny pot and the bullet in the tree and the button on the floor as the Shawnee drum (a present from the last Shawnee) was hacked in its middle so its belly ceased to pump. And we remembered the settler man and his words *stay* and *home* and *plant* which we never gave him a chance to say. And we wondered why it was we had to go out to beyond yet never learned to say good-bye?

One of us survived and every time he passes where we now lie, for we were buried in the end by soldiers from a fort, we call out to him. But he never answers.

What do we call out?

Why, Good-bye.

one   The flutes had played in his head since three weeks out of Santa Fe. Above the Kiowa wail of the wind. Above the booming moon.

Way north, where the trail stumbled against the sky, the Cheyenne drum started up again. *Rapaho . . . Rapaho . . .* it said his name, and now he hid himself. Behind nothing but the wind he hid himself and where he stood it was dark and he could not be seen, save as a buffalo rock hung with rags.

Rags of matted hair. Of fringe—some leather, some Injun beaded. Of bits of cloth stuck into holes of clothes. Frayed feathers, beads and bracelets shushed and rattled in the wind. A satin rose from some forgotten dancehall bustle quivered on one sleeve, a silver spoon with the initial M he took to be an H clanked softly against the fringe of his jacket where it was tied. The stolen black crepe from a coffin lid stuffed in his left boot (which was a good place to carry an extra just-for-the-hell-of-it-might-come-in-handy-sometime thing) rustled in the wind. The red-tipped eagle claw left from his Cheyenne days whistled in his right ear. He reached up to touch it now, to make certain that was what was whistling. He lost it sometimes. Had found it on saloon floors, in tipis, in beds,

11

among buffalo hides, when he was still bringing in hundreds of hides, even buried once one whole winter beneath a snowbank he fell into after drinking a gallon of Taos Lightning. But he always found the claw. It was like him as his skin was like him. And when the wind blew against him, as now, and the claw whistled he remembered being young and felt a Cheyenne pony twisting between his knees and raised the lance which was not there to lead warriors who were not there in a battle that had long been fought. Then he remembered, dropped his hand, and listened for the drum again.

A bird, ragged as he but black, came against him on the wind, its feet out, its wings beating to hold it back. Still it blew against him, clawed onto his shoulder and turned to face the wind, working its wings to hold on.

Both of them stood with the wind in their eyes and their mouths. Rapaho waiting for the drum to call again. The bird just waiting.

"Must be more'n one of us is all that I can say," he said, and that started him to giggling so that the bird flew away.

But the drum stopped. And there was only the mutter of dust. Buzzard shadows. Sun.

Then a rough-legged hawk *kreed* once above a herd of dust-stained bones where a smoke of buffalo gnats twitched up and down, their hungry eyes watchful for the bones to stand again, their brittle wings whistling, "Be alive!"

He turned and blinked at them.

"They's bulls somewhere," he answered. "They's alive somewhere."

The smoke of them blew against his eyes till all he could see was a greyness and all they could see were two shiny eyes. But grey. But old. Not buffalo eyes. The gnats twitched up again, hung over the bones, dropped to the trail and now he couldn't be sure what they whistled because of the muffling dust. But it sounded like, *"He don't know."*

"I do so know," he flushed. "Down by the Cimarron they's bound to be leben, seventy of the Texas herd. Get yourselves on down there. You can go. You ain't Wanted like me."

He stomped at the smoke of them till they rose and drifted south with the wind, leaving him staring at the yellow dust where the hot winds had burned a time or two or three. But then he heard the grass walking around, grass the hot winds hadn't touched, standing-up grass, brown maybe for it was August, but grass that was still alive. More alive than the dust.

He stared at it now, saw it wilting in the heat, then he closed his eyes and felt the earth drifting off with the gnats and the wind . . . going south . . . to the Cimarron . . . the Canadian . . . the swollen-tongued Yarner plains. And then he remembered that when he was young and lived with the Cheyenne he could ride a pony swinging from one arm, his strong brown fingers caught in the mane, the braided loop between his teeth while the ground went spinning every which way as his pony jumped dead men, broken tipis, fallen buffalo, prairie fires and sit-skidded down mountains. *Then* he was never dizzy. Why was it when he was young he could whip around thru the sky on a round-butted pony and never get dizzy. But now that he was old he had only to stand and watch the grass wilting in the heat and his whole head went off somewhere with the wind.

I ain't old, he thought with his eyes still squeezed tight. Haggis is dead and Chien went under a herd that was runnin and at Sweetwater someone said Joner died of thirst in California. But they was old men. Weak. Always weak. Not

13

like me. I'm still hard as a young bull . . . and I can't count my years nohow I was borned so many times . . . here and there . . . highland and low . . . green some and desert . . . tipis, trails, and girlhouses. Haggis'll tell you. He opened his eyes. No guess Haggis can't . . . no more. Reckon that makes me the last cibolero.

He'd always called himself a cibolero. But the ciboleros were long gone up the Salt with Haggis, their flat straw hats no longer keeping out the sun, their lances broken, their quivers of arrows lost, their straw stirrups dragging under their horses' bellies. In Santa Fe they called him a buffalo hunter. The traders called him a hide man. But he always said, "I'm a cibolero," and tapped his own straw hat to make sure they saw it and when they said, "But the ciboleros are gone," he said back, "*I* ain't."

He scratched his head with the Spanish skinning knife. It belonged in its velvet case in the wagon. But he was carrying the knife in his hand. For luck he was carrying it. He believed in luck. Other hunters didn't. They believed in put-up-a-herd, stand-and-shoot, run-them-if-you-got-to, kill. He believed in luck. Also the tiny doll of cornhusks, whang and buckeyes which he kept in with the skinning knives. Also charms, spells, songs. Also smoke. White hides. Tobacco. Eagle claws. Drums.

"I'll get my buffalo too," he turned and yelled after the smoke of gnats, dim in the yellow air. "I can call em, you know. Same as an Injun . . . learned from the Pawnee . . . or maybe the Sye-ox. . . ."

But he didn't call them.

"No use to call when they're still so far away . . . hid in some canyon . . . by some waller . . . by some world of grass. . . ."

He looked out to the north again. But there was nothing

14

new to see. Only the tired grass. A boulder here and there. A hill just standing. Buzzards circling with nothing else to do.

"Nothin to circle for either."

Just a lot of sun and grass and sky and not even a wallow, save one three days back, old and dried hard as the adobe clay of the ranch he'd lost to Blackjack Sunday in the poker game.

"Well," he thought it over for the hundredth time, "there was that Kiowa boy I went and shot anyway . . . so he is dead and soldiers ain't what they used to be . . . all out for the damn Injuns now . . . so I got to go huntin anyway."

He took off his split straw hat and flicked a lingering gnat from the brim. "Eye still good . . . coulda shot you you varmint," he yelled after it. "Coulda shot you down kickin and bellerin . . . if you could beller." He watched the gnat drift off with the wind. "Reckon you can kick," he added.

He stooped to read the sign in the grass, but his back caught around his left hip joint and he stood there, half up and half down, not trying to squat like he would have when he was young and wore only a breechcloth and had hard brown legs. "Ain't no need to crawl on the ground like a ant anyway."

But he waited a long time, half up half down, before the pain went away and he could stand up straight again.

"I'm hard as a rick." He frowned. "No . . . they've been known to break. Like a bull, then. No, they die bellerin. No . . . I'm more like a . . . like some kind of a mountain that never falls down and dies and gets busted. A mountain can stand millions of feets walkin on it and never get busted. Wind slammin against it. Sun stompin on it. Moon too."

He felt better then. He liked the picture of himself as a mountain and in his mind ran over the mountains he'd crossed, seen, slept on, fought on, killed on. He tried to pick out one to be his own. One to be him. Stony? Smooth? Hump-backed? Straight up and down? He couldn't decide and he quit trying when he saw the mule looking at him.

Wonder how far into a man's eyes that mule can see? he thought.

The mule knew him. The mule was old too. The mule knew how he was . . . how sometimes when he climbed down off the rickety wagon to read the sign he forgot the mule and wagon were with him and he went on walking into the wind. Winter and summer like the buffalo he followed the wind.

"Water . . ." he'd sniff when it was water they needed and move away from the wind if water wasn't hidden beneath it. "Injuns went by," he'd say and sniff out the tribes and their goings. "Fire," he'd say and sniff whether it was a prairie fire or a hunter's camp or some settler burning his field out west of Buffalo City that someone said was now called Dodge.

And the little mule would follow after him, dragging the wagon, stopping to work it over rocks or out of ruts when it hung up, because the mule knew the old man would go on walking and forgetting her for a long time maybe. The mule didn't want to just stand there in the sun, hitched to a wagon, and wait for the buzzards to drop down with the night and see she was helpless there and bound to the wagon. Or maybe for a wolf to come walking by from that tall stand of grass where it had been lying all day, watching and flicking its ears and staying cool while the mule sweated and grew weak from just standing there alone by herself in the sun.

The old man went on now, slowing as he started up a hill. The mule moved out too, eyed the hill, then stepped it up so

16

her hoofs were kicking up breaths of dust. The mule had been a wagon mule a long time, but she had run with Injun ponies. Clip-clip-clip-clip-clip and six miles an hour day and night she could make. For days and nights. Forever maybe. She had never had to try for forever.

At the start of the hill she passed the old man where he was dawdling along. She kept going. But slower and slower and slowing because the hill was steeper than the mule remembered hills when she was young. And she was just one mule where once she had had teammates and led eight wagons rolling over the prairie. And she was tired.

Halfway up the hill the mule faltered, the wheels slipped, and the old man, seeing it, leaned against the wagon and pushed. But soon he grabbed on the worn brake, and then he got some rocks and chocked the wheels and both man and mule just stood there, halfway up the hill. They just stood there, breathing hard in their chests where their hearts were breaking. They just stood there, listening to the brake groaning as it slipped a little. They just stood there, looking down . . . remembering.

"A hunderd wagons was mine," the old man muttered. "A hunderd fine new wagons made by a man who usta build boats on the coast of the east where they's a sea. Well," he lowered his voice to a mumble, "maybe it wasn't a hunderd." He looked at the mule, for she was looking at him. Wonder how high a mule can count, he thought and looked away, then closed his eyes to watch the fine new wagons creaking up the hill. Rough men at the reins. Proud skinners, outcasts of men who often camped apart from the others with their long Spanish knives in their shirts where their skins could keep them warm. Wild hunters and wiry scouts. Men carrying Comanche lead in their legs. Arrow scars on their chests. Scalpings in their eyes. Maybe a hungry

17

buffalo calf would be running among the wagons. A young calf whose mother they'd killed bawling alongside the young mules whose strength shook their flanks like the sound of going.

"It's all the day long we go trampin around
In search of the buff that we may shoot him down.
Our guns on our shoulders, our belts forty rounds,
We send em up Salt River to some Happy Hunting Grounds.
Our meat, it is the buffalo hump
Our . . . sleep . . . the girl's . . . hide . . . bed
We sleep the . . . goddam . . . sore thumb . . ."

He broke off.

"Boots?" he asked himself. And then he forgot the song altogether for it went out of his head on the wind and he was content to stand there in the sun and listen to the flutes whistling in his head.

"Is them flutes Cheyenne?" He rubbed his head. "Or maybe . . . did Cheyenne have flutes . . . or was it whistles . . . seems like there was somethin whistlin all the time. . . ."

He was part Spanish, part Cheyenne, part Comanche, part Chinese, part Kaintuck, "And I speak em all," he bragged. Well, some few words of all. He knew one Chinese word a Chinese laundryman had said down at Rath City when he dropped the sad iron on his foot. And as for the rest . . . he'd told so many lies, and drunk so much whiskey with the lies, and thought so many thoughts watching the skies, and tasted so much blood spurted into his face from the buffalo on the other end of the Big Fifty . . . he wasn't too sure just who he started out as. That's what he meant when he said he was born so many times. When he hit a stranger place where no one knew him, he just started in all over again and made up a new life to brag on . . . till he got careless and lost that one too. . . .

Was his ma really a Comanche and had his cradleboard swung from her saddle as the Comanches moved out on their winter hunt? He'd said as much many a time in some saloon while dusty-eared girls with dusty satin slippers, or none at all, and dusty red stockings, or none at all, and dusty painted faces, or none at all, stood around and grinned in the heat, glad to have just some old man to talk and break the weary fatigue of another monotonous day. Now he tried to go back and put himself in the cradleboard seventy years ago. But, he shook his head, he couldn't remember.

"Maybe she was Cheyenne," he said aloud. Then shook his head again and squinted up the hill where a stalk of grass was dancing faster than the rest so that some bug had seen it and was sneaking up its leaf.

"Course, that woman . . . that one I had the longest . . . that one that was always skinny and craved buffalo liver raw . . . that one I-killed-her-husband-by-the-waterhole . . . she was Comanche. Maybe," he scratched his head with the point of the skinning knife, feeling each pore with its flickering tip, "maybe that ain't right either."

He worked the knife round to the back of his head and scraped over the old scar where his hair teased the skin. A buffalo had got him there when he was still running with the Cheyenne. Whooping like a young coyote. Counting coup among the Crow. Cutting his pony into a buffalo herd to run them and shoot point blank as he came up beside them. He had a tall Blackfoot woman then and a red-haired scalp swung from his belt, the scalp of the young buffalo hunter he'd taken her from one night when the hunter wouldn't trade her for horses, gold or hides.

19

He looked at the mule.

"Well, Berthy Conchita . . . we're still standin here like fools."

And he took off the brake and the mule pulled and he pushed and they made it up into the hills where a storm was making out about the crest and the wind was whipping clouds in long white banners like a chinook wind, and, "If they's any of the Arkansas or Republic herd left . . . they's somewhere up here . . ." he told the mule. "Up here above the Yarner."

But the Yarner was behind them. Miles and miles it was behind them. He thought that over as he climbed back on the wagon and then he said, "By God . . . looks like the Yarner to me. By God . . . it's moved."

And he picked up the reins, hunched over, shut his eyes to shut out the stomping grass and soon he was smiling, seeing inside his head young warriors dancing to the flutes, the fires heaped up with buffalo tongues and humps, the Blackfoot woman nursing her babe.

That kid, he thought, he was lighter'n dark and his hair was curly like mine. That kid . . . must've been mine . . . wonder whatever come of him . . .

They wandered thru the rest of the day on the edge of the sprawled out hill, following an old drovers' trail that crossed older buffalo trails winding to water somewhere below. Sometimes he could count fifty buffalo trails, each hock deep in the ground. But no bulls had been on them of late. Nothing but ants and snakes. Beetles. Grasshoppers. Green headed flies.

Now he began to feel the pulse in the round hot buffalo eye that other men called the sky.

"Up here it ain't changed none," he said. "They's here all right."

20

The wind rumbled far off now and he could hear the hoofs of tall thin mustangs trampling it into the ground. The hunting wolves strangled their howls and fell on the fallen wind. The buzzards came down. The coyotes waited. The wind fought back and buffalo started up, shaking the earth.

"The wagons'll roll all night long," he said, and wrapped his tongue around the one eye tooth in his head and let the tip hang out in the sun.

"Them bulls'll set up a bellerin and a thunderin and a rumblin and you can hear their dew claws rattlin . . . rattlerattlerattle."

They were a lumpy brown silhouette now. The man, the mule, and the wagon. They walked a brown ridge against a brown sky on brown land. It was flat brown this time of day. No sharp shadows. No edges to anything. No real light. Just soft like a buffalo hide with the fur side out. They were both so tired they didn't hear the wagon creaking against the ruts and groaning over. Nor the mule's clip-clip-clip-clip and six miles an hour a day for forever. Nor their own breaths. All either of them was thinking was to go on till it was time to stop. But when did it come time to stop? Neither knew.

"Bout all you can say for such ground," he said, "is that you don't have to swim it. It don't offer much in way of praise."

The hot of the air began to go. The yellow was gone. It was the kind of light that a man who was plowing went on and plowed thru thinking it was still day, but a man who was sleepy went to bed thinking it was night.

Flashes of red began to come in the air like it might be making weather up somewhere ahead. Sometimes there was a purple glow. Sometimes it was grey. Then the air turned wet and, "We're close on to some river," he said.

21

He made camp on the edge of the hill downgoing and cooked a mess of beans. Then he sat very still and listened to the Cheyenne drum call again . . . *Rapaho-o-o-o-oo-ooo-o.*

The last doves had their say. The coyotes woke up for good. Below on the flats, he began to hear broken hide wagons thundering over rocks with their own kind of thunder. Men whistling at mules. Big Forty-four's and Fifties going off. Even in the dark, the big guns were going off and torches were riding up and down where a skinner went to the kill to work the hide before it stiffened.

"They's makin hides down there," he whispered, his grey eyes wide. "Think I won't know up here . . . but I do know."

The moon came up, stepped over the herd of bones in the flats. But even the moon couldn't fool him. "I know you're lyin," he yelled at it. And then he saw the herd standing, all hide and flesh and hair. Bawling and snorting. Running and falling. Dying. And *boom* went the moon and a big Forty-four and, "Makin hides!" he yelled.

Then he let the herd run off into the dark and saw again their bones.

"I can call em down anytime," he said at last. "I can call em down out'n the mountains and the hills, even down from the Salt with old Haggis and Chien and Joner to drive em and all them dead ciboleros a whoopin."

He laughed, his mouth open and dark save for the one eye tooth cold white in the moonlight.

Then he fell back and went to sleep with his hat still on and he dreamed of Haggis and Chien and Joner. Dreamed they were trying to pull off his boots. Dreamed it because his feet were hot and swollen and hurt and because he couldn't pull off his own boots with the pain in his hip. But after the boots were off and he could wiggle his toes in the air, he went on and dreamed he was where the flutes were playing and the drum was beating and he saw it was his son by the Blackfoot woman who was pounding the drum.

So that's what come of him.

Then he dreamed he was a boy wearing a rough leather shirt and he was washing his hands in a spring and right by his shoulder there was a jaybird calling. Behind him there was a cornfield all blue, deep blue and tassling. And way off someone was singing a song about everlasting arms.

Ain't my dream, he thought in his sleep and broke it off. *Belongs to someone else.* And he roused up and yelled, "Hey . . . hey keep your dreams to home."

Then he dreamed that the Cheyenne were starting out on their winter hunt but that iron rails were laid across their travois tracks where the silly little trains screeched up and down in the nights. Once they had only screeched in the days, the nights being too black and full of herds to travel. Now there was no need to stop. Telegraph poles stood by the empty wallows. Soldiers bobbed up and down everywhere with their yellow kerchiefs flying and their *Hooo-OOOOooo.*

But that made him wake again because it was no dream and was true. Nothing was the same as in the old days except that when the sun was tired of burning hot it would turn south and winter would come on. Only this did not fail.

After a long time he went to sleep again and he dreamed he was following a wagonload of mixed breeds because they were carrying black powder and he wanted them to blow up the government because he had the feeling that if the government were gone, the buffalo would come back.

In his dream he thought he made it very clear to the Indians:

A man can't get a good night's sleep for them damn

23

things, he'd told the breeds as he waved toward a wheezing train. *Them damn things is everywhere you want to be that buffalo should be.* But they had looked at him with dumbness in their black eyes as if they didn't understand his words. *Bobwire,* he said. But the driver of the wagon only fingered the reins and looked past him while the one beside him who carried an old gun yawned and went to sleep. *I still kin set a charge,* he said, *remember from my minin days . . . and there they'll go . . . the goddam gov'mint . . . whoops and bang and there they'll go.*

He woke again and decided that the Injuns in his dream hadn't known what the government was and that was why they didn't hurry to blow it up. He didn't know exactly what it was either, except that sometimes some Sye-ox came along with a coin dangling from his neck and saying things like *Great White Father,* and he thought the government was some kind of man, yet more than that for it had its fingers into everything so that a man had no freedom at all as it was always taking land away and giving it to this one and to that one so when you'd been wandering a year the land had all changed hands just like in a poker game. That's likely what the government was, he thought, some crooked poker game that went on and on and some of the men who played in it were professional cardmen and some were sharpers who carried small derringers and some were stupid and didn't even know how to play but were just sitting in for someone else.

"And that is why there is telegraph poles all over where you want to hunt and where they isn't telegraph poles they is railroads and bobwire, so naturally a man can't find no buffalo and the government is lyin when they say we've killed em all."

He settled that and finally slept again. But when he did

24

he dreamed he heard a buffalo calf bawling in the hills and when the moon brushed against it he saw it had turquoise hoofs and sky-blue fur, not hair but fur, and its tiny horns were carved and set with gold inlay.

Now there is a calf.

But even in his sleep he knew the calf that he heard bawling was a mangy maverick he and Berthy Conchita had passed three days before grazing alongside an old old cow whose hair couldn't hide the scars of her years and whose herd were the bones that were scattered on the flat of the land below the camp.

Thought the coyotes would've pulled em down by now.

The moon climbed higher. It made shadows under the trees and rocks. The stars walked along, looking sleepy on toward dawn. Even in his sleep he saw them. And he finally roused again and said, "Couple more hours . . . gonna get up . . . call me down a herd." And then he really slept.

The little mule moved away from him to sweeter grass where a stream was running. Often she looked out over the hill where she could hear crickets along the Goodnight-Loving Trail that ran someplace she did not wonder about. Often she shook her head and held her nose to the windless air, not knowing that already from Dodge to Santa Fe everyone was talking about such a windless year. Often she lifted her head while chewing to stare at the yellow moon.

She nickered once at a herd of mustangs she could hear crossing the flats below. And then she lay down under the silent moon where the buffalo ran no more in the month of August. And she felt old.

two   The grave by the trail was old. The rocks on it were older. They had sunken into the ground with spring rains and winter snows. The grass grew up between them. They no longer showed where the hunger-weakened paws had clawed that first year. They were settled now not to be shifted again. Not to be snuffled. Licked. The body beneath must be dust at last or the paws would be clawing still. Perhaps the claws were dust as well.

Fallen across the rocks was a cross made from the ribs of a Conestoga. It had begun to crack apart a long time ago. On the crosspiece there had been a name once, stick-written with pitch from the bucket slung under every wagon. It was maybe a woman's name, for the marks were loopy, far apart. A man would have just one name and maybe an initial. *Merry Annabelle Elizabeth MacFarland*—it might have been that. Rapaho didn't know. He just made it up.

We'll bury her here, toppa this bluff . . . then we hafta get on.

Yes, that's prob'ly what they said, Rapaho thought.

We'll stick er down in here . . . then we hafta get on. They's signal fires and Kiowas coyotin in them hills.

Was that about what they said? he wondered. But it was just a passing wonder. Like most of his wonders. Just passing. Here it comes. There it goes. Gone. He didn't really care. It was not him shoveled under the fallen cross.

Graves is a silly waste, he thought. Whyn't they let the coyotes have her?. She mighta done some good. On the other hand, he thought again, she's done some good, she makes a fine trail mark.

More night fog blew between him and the grave. Now it was just a sort of lump. A sort of shade. A sort of I-am-here . . . where-are-you feeling that crept to him thru the dripping fog.

And then he heard the moon boom softly once and smiled that he was still alive. You're wrong, he nodded toward the grave. It's me that's here and you that's where. And he listened for the moon again, but it did not come again.

He sat cross-legged on the high wagon seat where he could see the plain when the light came over it again. A coarse Navajo rug was wrapped around him, its white grey and its red black and its black not even showing. He was hatless. The hat he'd left by the fire so the fire would know he was coming back. He was bootless too.

> *"De dum de dum de dum dee dee . . .*
> *AND with the faithful make a start*
> *To cross the PLAINS in your handcart."*

Dreamed about a handcart . . . no, never did neither . . . was the wagon . . . surround . . . herd of buffalo.

"Well, Mr. Rapaho," he said, "just what you reckon was that dream about?"

Once he could have said. When he was still a young man, still with the Cheyenne. Then he had taken his dreams to the medicine man, the one with buffalo horns and eagle wings and four yellow scalps hanging from his bird-claw

27

necklace. He had taken his dreams and handed them over. "What do they mean?" he had asked. But after that everything went wrong and he almost got killed among the Crow. And he was sorry he'd taken his dreams to the medicine man. That spring when the ponies got fat on the new grass, he had dressed four of his finest in feathered masks, braided their tails part way, tying the ends in a knot with a feather fastened to a buckskin cord, painted red hands on the shoulders of each (for each had ridden over the enemy with him on its back) and hung small brass bells in the slits of their ears. He took the ponies to the medicine man to buy back his dreams. Then maybe it would stop—the trouble. The fear. The almost getting his skull split in the night by a Crow axe. But the old man hid between his buffalo horns and said he couldn't find them. He said they must've gotten out and the dogs ate them. *Ai . . . the dogs are always hungry*. Rapaho had had to wait till he could catch the old man alone out on the prairie singing to some god. Then he caught him. Pegged him in sun. Took away the medicine bag and shook it out and saw all the sacred things no man was supposed to see. He unwrapped all the things from their hide coverings and their fur pouches and their bead lacings and their straw skins. He spread them out in the sun by the medicine man and he sniffed them, tasted them, listened for a voice that would cry out in a dream. But the dreams were really gone. Maybe stolen. Maybe sneaked away. Maybe found by some enemy who was using them against him. Maybe even dead. And if dead . . . maybe buried. He had killed the medicine man there in the sun and left him with the bits of birds, tobacco, teeth, claws, paint, dried mice, cut-off fingers, bones about him. And he had killed the four ponies because he thought some of the medicine man's evil had come down on them. And he had burned his lodge and gone away forever from the Cheyenne.

But even now, he still wondered, What happened to them dreams? And he wished he had them back, for maybe with those dreams and with his magic and his spells he could call the buffalo down.

"But I am gonna call em down," he said. "Mr. Rapaho, what you think we're doin sittin here up on this wagon in the night and fog when the fire'd be so much nicer and a sleep so much better. Mr. Rapaho, pay attention, please."

The fog made his hands cold. They could never squeeze the trigger of the Big Fifty across his lap. He pushed his hands in with the gun under its leather wrap and sought warmth from the barrel. Many's the time in the winter when he was bringing the buffalo down with the frost cloud above them and their beards dripping icicles he had jerked off his gloves and warmed his hands on the barrel of the gun. And it would be hot. The skin would burn. And his hands would be so cold he wouldn't feel the burning or know about it till later when the skin turned pink and hurt and began to peel from white blisters. But now there was no warmth from the barrel. It was cold like him.

"Well, Mr. Rapaho," he said, "let's us think back on how it is you call em down."

It had been a long time. Twenty-five . . . maybe thirty . . . No, couldn't be thirty . . . more like twenty . . .

"Well, Mr. Rapaho, we was took by the Pawnee when we was yonder to twenty, maybe fifteen, maybe only fifteen and we was only there a few months and now we're nigh onto seventy . . . no, more like fifty . . . more'n that, maybe sixty . . . couldn't be seventy . . . no man lives to be seventy, we must be around sixty-seventy but if we *was* sixty and was took when we was fifteen that would be about fifteen-twenty-five-thirty-five-forty-five-fifty-five and add another five and that would make it . . . no, take off another ten and that would make it forty-five. . . . *forty-five years.*"

He frowned and started over again, but no matter how many times he counted it on his fingers it still came out forty-five. But that couldn't be. No man got so old that things in the past were that far behind him.

"My God!"

He shivered suddenly. The chill was heavy on the air. The Navajo rug didn't keep him warm. The rug had once been brighter, newer. Then it had kept him warm. But he had been brighter, newer, too. He pushed at his hat. It hung so wet over his eyes he couldn't even see the fog. The feathers of it drooped. The eagle claw dripped water under his collar where the Cavalry handkerchief was tied to keep his neck warm, but he should have known it wouldn't. It was a government handkerchief, and the government was always the same. Out for the damn Injuns and settlers and trains and bobwire and never taking any care of its own. To hell with the gov'mint, he thought. And then his mind wandered off again. His mind was a strayer, a mustang rustling for forage and coming up with everything it couldn't eat but had to chew on anyway.

Oh, don't you remember sweet Betsy from Pike . . ."

He rocked back and forth now that the song had popped into his mind.

"*Who crossed the big mountains with her lover Ike*
With two yoke of oxen, a large yaller dog,
A tall Shanghai rooster and one spotted hog."

It don't make no sense to take one hog and one rooster and no hens, he thought. *One hen* woulda been better. If sweet Betsy or her lover'd had any sense they'd took two hogs and a hen. You can't get no eggs out'n a rooster, and you can only eat him once. Course, maybe a *Shanghai* rooster is different. Things is sometimes strange. Maybe a Shanghai lays eggs. Maybe it's a gov'mint rooster.

A   tall   Shanghai   rooster. How tall? Like dog-size tall? Boy-size tall? Man-size tall? That would be a tallllll rooster. He looked and tried to see it standing there beside him. He saw it as something painted on a buffalo robe. He made its eyes blue and the feathers of its tail yellow and purple polka dots with calico flowers of pink. Then he gave it wings like a butterfly with lots of veins and spots and shiny places. Lots of glitter. Lots of dew-like softness. Lots of sky-like shine. Then he gave it wattles like grass stems when they are wet and claws of silver with spurs of whittled gold nuggets.

Reckon a rooster like that *might* be worth horsein across the country.

And his mind rustled on and came up with his gold running days and silver digging days and piles of dirt and water dripping from a rotten sluice and then his mind dropped that and went back to *Sweet Betsy from Pike.*

"Oh, don't you remember . . ."

He tapped his fingers softly on the wagon seat. The taps went out like a telegraph key and, *Here comes the news . . . listen . . . it's workin, Rapaho . . . the line is workin. You kin turn in your mochila . . . you won't be ridin for the Pony Express no more (nasty laugh).* And tiptaptaptiptaptiptiptiptaptiptapclicketyclickety. What does it say? *It says, They's been a massacre.* You're a liar. It don't say nothin. It says tipatapatip. Just because you think I'm only

31

a ignorant hunter, too old to ride for the Express and too loose-footed to keep a Station . . . By God, I am so a rider . . . they ain't all fifteen years old! No one kin ride better'n me. Not even a Comanche!

"He was a dern fool not to answer me with his mouth steada his damn keys."

And he went on tapping his fingers against the seat as the keys had gone on tapping even after the man who knew what they said lay dead by the kerosene lamp whose wick was spluttering in the oil and whose chimney was smoking so that the room darkened and tipatapatip while the dust blew on the door and around its edge to spatter the soles of the dead man's boots and creep clear up to the hands he had kept so proudly scrubbed.

"He was a fool."

He looked up. Dawn was coming. The fog was getting lighter. It was time to call them down, the buffalo. But he couldn't remember how.

I do so remember how, he told himself. Why, I couldna forgot. All the hide men west of the Mississippi usta beg to hunt with me cause I could call em down. Summer or winter. No matter where we stopped. Why . . . we'd pick nice places with sweet water nearby and good wind shelter and lots of grass for the horses and mules, places where other hide men wouldn't go cause they said they wasn't no buffalo for miles and miles, maybe hunderds of miles clear up and down and east and west. We'd get dug in and get our stuff scattered around till it looked like we'd lived there all our lives and scout around for sign and drink a lot of Taos Lightning and cuss and dance and fight some . . . His mind trailed off and over hundreds of camps in hundreds of places in what seemed like hundreds of years, and when it came back he'd forgotten about calling them down and

32

was thinking instead of the White Russian skinner who was such a mean fighter.

"And that's why he's dead," Rapaho said.

A dove called now. He sighed and quit tapping the seat. He turned to crane to the east. It was getting day now. It was kind of yellow thru the fog. Kind of pinkish, greenish, yellow.

"Mr. Rapaho," he said, "we gotta remember."

But the fog began to thin and the light began to brighten and a hawk was up flying.

I gotta remember now because I'm feelin tired and old though-I-ain't-old but feelin tired's the same and I-ain't-got no place to live and don't know nobody to take me in and anyway I never begged.

His hands were shaking now.

Winter's gonna come and I can't stay out here not anymore alone like-I-usta. I can't stand to stay out anymore cause-cold-air-hurts-me-all-the-time coughin-and-sneezin till I like to jerk my guts out of my mouth and I just got- ta MAKE HIDES. I just gotta have somethin to take back with me to take back with me to-take- back-with-me.

"Hey there, Rapaho . . . hey there . . . I got a job for you. You know them buffs you been killin all these years . . . well, they's all gone, but we shorely to God got us a good market for bones. If you wanta go out and fetch em in, I'll buy em from you. . . ."

"I wonder at what?" Rapaho asked himself. "At what was that stingy boneman gonna buy em? Hunderd dollars? No. More'n likely fifty. No, not him. Twenty-five. And by the time I lay in grub and track myself out and walk myself out and the mule too I'd likely make a grand profit of five whole cents."

His hands held each other now. His hands were all he had to hold onto now, and they were all each other had.

"Well, I'd think you'd be damn glad. I'd think you'd be damn glad for any kind of work that'd make a livin. Hell, you're a old man. You killed em. Why shouldn't you go out and pick their bones? Look at it this way—it's kinda like you been puttin money in the bank all these years since you killed em but now you kin still go out and make more money off of em just pickin their carcosses and it's easy work cause they're already dead and just layin there waitin. Hell man, it's easier than bein a buzzard and havin to strip the meat off. They ain't nothin *to* strip. Just old bones to pick up."

His hands hurt bad now. He thought one of his little fingers was bending to break. But still he held tight, rocking back and forth.

"I'll tell you one thing . . . if I was down to one mule and a bustedy wagon and standin round saloons with my tongue hangin out just hopin some feller'd offer me a drink, I shorely to God wouldn't be too damn proud to go out and pick them bones."

His face darkened. He was ashamed that he had remembered that. Even though Haggis and Chien and Joner were dead and not there to see it, he was ashamed. He twisted his toes around now. Just holding his hands wasn't enough.

"Hey there, Rapaho . . . old hunter . . . best hunter that ever was . . . best hunter in the whole damn west . . ." he mimicked the boneman's voice, "brought in more hides than any livin man . . . or dead man for all that. Hey there

34

old man . . . go out and pick me up some b   o
n   e   s. Go out there like a goddam bobwire settler and fetch em back to me . . . fetch em boy . . . fetch em
. . . fetch back the bones . . . fetch em back and I will give
you FIVE CENTS A TON.

"Hey there, Rapaho . . . Mr. Rapaho . . . go out and work
your tail off in the August sun pickin up bones . . . tire
out your legs that catch with ever step as you pick up them
bones . . . get down on your knees old man and crawl along
like a goddam snake, get down, down boy down, lower
down and pick pick pick them bones till you're so damn
low you're crawlin on your hair and I WILL GRANDLY AND
GENEROUSLY GIVE YOU FIVE WHOLE CENTS A TON. Because I
am a kind man. Because I am a good man. Because I am a
rich merchant. I got lots and lots of money and slabs of
bacon and ain't your mouth just waterin and pounds and
pounds of coffee and barrels of flour and sugar and kegs
of molasses and sacks of beans and see this here new coat
that just come in on the stage from Chicago, and ain't it
purty with that fine furry collar on it to keep a man's ears
warm when the wind's a blowin. That's the last one with a
collar like that. That's the last of the fur. Yessir, that's what
the drummer said. That's the last we'll be seein out here.
And you kin have it if you pick up enough bones and then
won't matter how cold the winter gets cause you got bones
to pick up old man . . . and more bones . . . even the Cheyenne bones (remember the Sand Creek massacre?) and I'll
take wolf bones too, even buzzard bones and if you find
any graves you might dig em up and fetch them bones
along. Just fetch em in and keep a fetchin em in you lucky
bastard to be able to pick up bones for me who eats steak
and eggs ever day and follers with whole pots of coffee."

I sold him hides for years, Rapaho thought, breaking off

35

the memory of the man's voice. I put him in business. With the hides I brung in year in year out I put him in business. I made it possible for him to eat his eggs and steak and drink his coffee, and when I go in and try to borry a little beans and coffee and sugar and flour on credit and a little tiny bit of gunpowder and a few bullets, what do I get? He tells me to go out and pick up goddam bones!

He let his hands and toes go suddenly. They were aching hard. My God, what if I've really broke somethin? he thought. When I was young it wouldn't have mattered none. Then, I coulda walked nine days on a broke leg till it healed and never knowed no pain . . .

Hey there, Rapaho . . . it's better'n starvin . . .

> *"Pickin up bones to keep from starvin*
> *Pickin up chips to keep from freezin . . .*
> *Way out yonder in no man's land . . ."*

"I'll never pick up that first goddam bone. Never. First I'll go back to the Cheyenne. Nothing is ever gonna happen to them. Even on reservations. Hell, reckon I could live on a reservation. Plenty of em would say I'm fullblood. Why, there's Spotted Calf and Stone Eater and White Turkey Runnin On The Ground. No, I heard they was dead. Well, they's Old Horse . . . no, he's dead . . . I saw him on the scaffold. Well, they's . . . hell they's someone!"

The sun was really coming on now. The fog yellowed more. There was a dazey light over everything. The fog hung and swayed like it was caught on bobwire. But it wasn't. He looked away from the ghosty glow and felt comforted when the mule blew nearby.

They is such a thing as   a   man   goin beyond   his   time... .

But then he heard the running feet. Somewhere. Nearby. Closer.

A herd.

It took him four tries to get to his feet. On his feet he heard them better. They were really coming on. He held hard to the brake and listened with his head cocked to one side and his hair yanked back from his good ear where the eagle claw was silent in the fog.

But where're they runnin?

He blinked into the dazey yellow light. No shapes nor shades were there. Then up above he saw them, saw them passing over, somewhere between the end of the sky and the earth. They made no sound a plain man could have heard. No, only a hunter could have heard them. Their mouths were open to bellow, but did not. Their tongues lolled, but nothing dripped from them. Their wild eyes rolled, but did not focus. They came up one side of the sky and went down the other. Hard behind them ran Cheyenne ponies with Cheyenne riders in the fog that now was brighter and seemed to drive them even faster so that he called to the sun, "Don't come . . . you'll drive em off . . . hold back . . ." But the sun came on and dulled the herd.

"Damn!" he yelled at the sun, and fell down off the wagon and tried to run ahead of the spreading light with the Big Fifty in his arms, and as he ran he called to the Cheyenne riders to circle them and when they didn't, whistled for the ponies to bring them around, and whistled and whistled *Turn them.*

But the riders who were not hunters lay low over their ponies' backs with not an arrow drawn. They lay low over their ponies' backs as if they were sleeping. And the ponies ran with their necks straight out, not arched and working hard. They ran in a steady long run that meant they were going on forever and their eyes were glazed and fastened on something he could not see. The herd passed over him in the hundreds . . . thousands . . . thousand thousands and as the light grew brighter he saw that at their head ran a buffalo calf with hoofs of turquoise and eyes of diamonds. And he fell back and was afraid because it was the same calf of his dream.

Pain came up in his throat and his jaws ached and his heart began a terrible pounding. He fell slowly, dropping the Big Fifty as he fell, and it went off, blasting a hole in the ground and kicking up pebbles and dirt into his face. But he never felt it. He lay face down, then rolled to see the herd and watched them running west . . . heading west . . . trying to beat the sun . . . running from the sun . . . making for California and the sea and the China coast where his granddaddy, he often said, had eaten rice and drunk tea in the mornings before going out to hunt and his grandmammy had worn three pearls in a red silk bag around her neck.

He came and went inside himself, as if some part of him were trying to get loose and follow after them, but the other part which was heavy, the part which moved and was alive and felt the pain in his throat, the part which was old and worn out and covered with scars and wrinkled skin, it held back and finally the other part which had wanted to go with them fell back within the heavy part and together they watched the sky turning green, then peach, then gold, then blue. Just before it turned blue he thought he saw Haggis and Chien and Joner at the tail of the herd and maybe two-three ciboleros with broken straw hats.

"Our buffalo who art in heaven . . .
With the tall Shanghai rooster and one
spotted hog

Hallowed be thy bones
Comeback be thy name . . ."

The throat pain was deep and choking and his fingers twitched against it.

The mule was curious when full day with its white sky came and still he lay where she had seen him fall. She went over to him and nickered once. Shoved him with her head and heard him moan. Brayed. But after a while she forgot him and went to stand on the edge of the bluff and look out to the west where a dust cloud was settling and something was running by. She nickered, but there was no answer. And finally she went back to the sweet grass and rolled under the morning sun.

Neither of them saw the small shape of a buffalo calf on the hill above, which stood for a long time against the sky watching them.

three It was there when he woke next morning. The buffalo calf. It stood on one side of him with its nose hanging over his shoulder.

"For Crissake," he said and closed his eyes again.

The mule raised her head when he spoke and stared at him. She also stared at the calf. The mule knew about buffalo calves alone. She had pulled the wagons with the wet hides of the cows thrown on and the calves running beside and bawling. She heaved in her chest and went back to eating.

"Berthy Conchita," he said after a while, "is that damn thing still here?" And when she didn't answer with a rumble from her chest, he sneaked another look. But it was still standing beside him only its nose was a little closer to his shoulder.

"That is the ugliest calf I ever seen," he said, and then he shut his mouth and eyes and lay very still and even tried to keep his chest from moving with his breaths. He thought if he were quiet and didn't move it might go away, because he knew about the lone calves too and he knew that they would follow anything that moved when their ma's were dead and he didn't want it following him. But it didn't go

40

away. It bawled in a cracked voice sort of way and kept on standing right beside him.

"Run it off, Berthy Conchita," he said and waited to hear the mule do as he had told her. The mule could do things like that when she wanted to. At least that's what he said down at Santa Fe, though no one had ever seen her do anything he told her. But when he heard the mule still pulling grass he opened his eyes again, and the calf was still there looking at him and waiting for him to get up.

"What you think," he said, "that I'm gonna feed you? Get away."

He thought he would sleep again and when he woke the calf would be gone to the same place where the dreams went. But the flutes started up in his head again and the Cheyenne drum set up a booming and a calling and the wind began to blow in under his lashes till he could feel it rolling around in the pupils of his eyes and he remembered that he hadn't called them down and he hadn't any hides and he was old...

No, I *ain't* old.

"Well," he said to the calf to keep himself from thinking of the night and dawn and buffalo rushing thru the sky, "whereat's your ma?" And then he said, "How kin I ask you such a dumb thing as whereat's your ma when I don't think you're smart enough to understand a word I say."

He sat up slowly, pulling and pushing with his arms, and the calf stepped back a little and tossed its head to clear his shoulder. "Well, you got more sense than I thought," he said. He focused his good eye on the calf to see if it were any use to shoot it for the hide, though he hardly thought it was, else he wouldn't have passed it up before. But it wasn't any use to waste the shot. Its ribs stuck out so hard and stiff the hide looked worn where they rubbed. Its knee bones stuck out too. Its mane was pitiful. Its head was smaller than it should have been. Its coat was ratty. Its boss was thin and poor.

"You look like you just got borned," he told it, "but ain't no calves dropped in August. What kinda calf are you? I never seen such a made thing in my life." He reached out for its head suddenly and tried to pry open its mouth; the memory of buffalo tongues roasting by a fire was hot in his mind. "Open up," he said. "Lemme see your tongue."

But the calf wrangled and fought with him and kicked him where his hip was always sore and he let go.

"Couldn't be no better'n the outside of you anyway."

The calf moved apart from him and stood with its head down as the mule did when she was pouting. Rapaho made a face at it. He picked up a stone and threw at it. He got the best breath that he could suck in and howled like a coyote. The coyote howl brought it to him when it should have driven it off.

"Crissake," he said, "don't you know nothin?"

He shoved at it and stumbled to his feet, which took a while as the calf kept knocking him over, for though it was small it was quicker than he.

"Don't you know I'm a hunter?" he said. "Don't you know I've got a gun that'd blow you up the Salt? Don't you know I've killed better'n you with nothin but my hands? Dumb thing . . . git!"

After he was on his feet and the ground quit leaping up and down and the wind stopped being a shaking thunder in his ears, he walked hopefully to the edge of the cliff and looked to see if there just might possibly be a herd that the calf belonged to. But even as he did he knew no herd was there, save the dead herd which had danced all night

42

and died all night but which now lay again like hard white flowers where the hot winds had passed.

He turned back from the cliff and looked again at the calf.

"Whereat is your ma?" he asked it, and shaded his eyes from the sun to stare out over the southern plain where he'd first seen the calf and cow. But there was no humpy dot grazing there and no bellowing that would mean she'd missed her calf. "Prob'ly some coyotes got her," he muttered to himself, "or some dumb settler seen her and killed her for her hide . . . yeah, some settler never seen a decent buffalo likely killed her for her hide . . . be lucky 'f it brings ten cents."

He made his way back to the wagon and he felt better now that some of the waking up stiffness was going from his joints, so that he stooped real quick like a young man and snatched up the Big Fifty and raised up without a catch anywhere. He found his hat and put it on after straightening its feathers and blowing at its crown. Then he climbed up on the wagon and flicked the reins.

"*Adios,*" he said to the calf. "And good luck to you."

But when he looked back the calf was trailing after, walking in the dust of the wagon and grunting pig-like, taking the wagon for its ma. He flipped the reins harder to make the mule clip faster so she stopped and stood there with her head down and her ears flopped over and the calf came up with them again. This time he climbed down from the wagon and gave Berthy Conchita a kick and her head swung around as she looked at him with interest. It wasn't often she got a kick, though there'd been plenty in the old days, and she was so surprised she took a step and he hurried to pull himself back on the wagon and grab the reins and hunch forward to brace himself against the wagon's sway.

43

But she stopped. She lowered her head and began to graze. He gave her another jerk with the reins and her head came up, but her eye rolled. She knew him. She threw her head and waggled her ears as if something were ahead of them like Cheyenne, and when she felt the slack come in the reins as he let them drop she rolled her eye backwards to see what he was doing. He was standing up on the seat of the wagon with his hat pushed back, staring ahead to see what had spooked her.

"Whatever spooked you, Berthy Conchita?" he said.

And she bobbed her head so that he put both hands up above his eyes to shade them to see better. He was settled now. Busy now. He would be staring to the north for an hour or more, she knew. And when he climbed down from the wagon and started walking ahead of her, she began to graze again.

The man and the mule knew each other's ways so well one often tricked the other.

Ever so often the mule would raise her head and look after him as he became a smaller speck against the sky. She chewed slow and loud now that he was out of hearing. It was early yet. If he didn't come back she'd follow. She had only to chew and drag the wagon as she pleased, for in this stretch there were no rocks to catch under the wheels nor cover for coyotes.

"I don't see nothin," he turned and yelled to her.

And then he squatted down, wanting to get back to the wagon, but it was far behind, so he waved his hat at the mule and yelled, "Come on." Then he prepared to wait for her to graze in his direction, and sat down hard and scratched his head and said, "She'll be along after while . . . grass this way's better."

He closed his eyes and dozed, but the calf came grunting

up to him and tried to suck on a feather of his hat and he raised up and shoved it back and yelled "Come on, Berthy Conchita, for Crissake."

When the wagon came up with him he climbed on, picked up the reins, and sat, not noticing they were not moving.

Hawks rose and fell across the sky. Shadows moved from one side of things to the other. He dozed again as he sat on the wagon. The day went on without him. Ever so often the mule took a step and the wagon jolted but he didn't feel it. His head would bob on his neck a little and he would mumble something in his sleep, but didn't wake. The mule would look back sometimes to see that he was still there. The calf kept up with the wagon and it grazed out to one side where the mule hadn't gotten the grass. Sometimes it would come up to the wagon and rub its head against the side. Once it approached the mule, but the way she flipped her ears it stepped back.

It was near sundown when Rapaho woke again. The flutes started up with his wakening. The drum too. The wind. The moon was coming up on his right even though it was still broad day. He studied the moon and thought it was coming up in the wrong place.

"But that's your business," he said to it.

They were on the edge of a hill they hadn't made before. He looked down below and saw a field of beans that looked pretty sick though there was a sweet stream of water hard against it. There were a few cottonwoods standing here and there. A crooked line of buffalo bushes. Three or four wild plum trees. And there was something about the field and the trees that made him squinch up his eyes and try to remember and then he did.

"Why, Mr. Rapaho," he said, "we've put up this place

45

before from way back in the Injun days and Dragoon days and..."

He strained now to see what he knew was there. But the little sod house built into the hill was hidden. The house had been there almost as long as Rapaho could remember. Things came and things went and he lived one life, then another, made promises to be broken, meant to remember this or that, but forgot. But the little house he remembered.

In the years he'd been wandering up and down the land he had stopped by the little house several times. But no one was ever there. He had beat on the door. But no one ever answered. He had once opened the door. But there was nothing there he wanted to take. He could tell the house had sunken more into the ground now, for the hill was pressing lower against it. The roof and hill joined now. The old cottonwood which had been a whip when the house was built had fallen across the roof. It stayed there. The yard was always dusted with a broom. There were always a few chickens cackling about. Sometimes other things, once a hog.

"By God ... telegraph poles, bobwire, railroad tracks and the damn gov'mint ... but this ain't changed," he chuckled. "Bet he thinks it's hid. Well, he had his chance that time the bounty hunter was after me ... so I don't bother him none."

And he sat there for a long time while the mule tossed her head and nickered and the calf grunted and the buzzards crossed the hills, for there were things he knew ... things he knew ... things he knew....

four

The shadows turned longer. His stomach began to hurt from being empty. He reached back in the wagon for something to chew and came up with dried beans. He tried them and they were musty. He spit them out and chewed on tobacco instead.

"Stomachs ain't got no sense," he said. "They'll eat anything and think it's food. It's only mouths got sense."

Now they moved back toward the camp and ever so often he turned to see if the calf still plodded after them. But it was always there. Its coat dustier. Its small eyes duller. Its thin legs shakier. And everytime he looked at it he said, "Such a ugly calf!"

He could remember such beautiful ones, such fat yellow ones just born, and such lively red ones with their new hair showing just an edge of color that when grown would mean they'd be called a beaver after their color.

"Sold many in my day for seventy-five dollars when all else was fetchin three."

Then there were the blue calves with long wool, and the russets and the black-and-tans and the white ones which were so rare that Injuns had killed hide men for them.

After he had looked back over the herds he'd known, the herds he'd killed, the beautiful calves that were dancing by the Salt, he turned again to the little calf wheezing at the dust thrown up by the wagon and shook his head.

"Crissake."

The drum started up again ahead of them and he slanted his eyes at the sound. It was just over the rim of the land. In his mind he saw it as a great yellow drum beating and pounding alone with no man's hand to pound it because it was the giant heart of all the buffalo he had killed. He felt its throbbing even in his boots. And where it tore the air apart it made the dust stand up in devils. And now it said not Rapaho, but *Hetanevo . . . Hetanevo . . . Hetanevo.*

He had not heard the name since he was a young buck living in the discarded top of a wealthy chief's lodge. And he remembered that when he was a young man he had leaned against the sky. Made a fast. Stood rigid for two days, three nights. Braced his back against the rain. Tasted the stars dripping onto his tongue. Smelled the musk scent of the very female earth. Heard the thunder thunder out beyond Orion. Dreamed up a white wolf with ears pierced with painted feathers, paws of straw, blue beads trailing from its tail where icicles swung. Chanted. Moaned. Howled at Mars. Felt no hunger, weariness, nor thirst. Saw a man whipping a mustang cloud. Called himself Hetanevo.

"Maybe," he said squinting into the sun, "it's a sign it's comin back . . . all I lost . . . and I ain't gonna be tired no more."

But when they stopped at a rill for water and he clambered off the wagon and knelt to drink between the mule and calf, there was an old man in the water looking back at him with the shine gone out of his eyes. Old hair white and blowing in the wind. Old skin wrinkled and scarred and blotched by sun. Old bones standing out like skinning

48

knives. And he and the old man studied each other while a spider walked across their noses and a buzzard flew behind their heads and a cloud rested against their hats. Then he leaned back, the water bitter on his tongue.

"I don't think he's comin back," he said. "I don't think that whoopin young varmint that I remember is ever comin back."

And when he climbed back up in the wagon the shadow of the old man hung onto his leg.

The mule started off without being told and Rapaho swayed on the seat and stared out with pain around his mouth.

The flutes began whirring loudly now. With sundown they seemed to gain more strength. The moon began to burn and it made a few soft booms. The stars broke thru the sky. He turned the wagon toward Arky who shone brightly in the west. But when they got to camp he was asleep again and dreaming that the sky was filled with buzzards with long black tails like fringe. And behind them came eagles and nighthawks and butterflies and they were words to songs he knew. And he went on and dreamed he heard a rumbling in the earth and then a herd came out of the sky, making for him.

Their hoofs were fire from the mountains of copper and iron and gold. Where they had been running across the mountains the metal had clung to their hoofs and hung in dribbles like tears and jingled as they ran with a sound that had no pain of spurs about it. Their coats were fur instead of hair and they were all colors. This fur that was their coats swayed back and forth, a sort of spangled fringe, a sort of spangled willow fringe, a sort of spangled spider's fringe. Their horns were carved by many winds in the designs of things the buffalo know, such as stars and moons

49

and suns and trees and flowers. Their eyes were jewels, rubies, emeralds, sapphires and many other stones he did not know.

At their head ran a calf with turquoise hoofs and horns inlaid with gold and eyes of diamonds and fur that was the blue of all the skies he'd seen.

They bellowed as they ran a kind of music that could never be sung or whistled but only carried in his head like the sound of wind. And as they came down on him, the calf lifted him on its back and he knew then they were all the buffalo that he had killed and behind him he could hear Haggis and Chien and Joner driving them on and the dead ciboleros whistling. Then they left the earth and climbed into the sky where O'Ryan waited beside his ricks.

He woke there on the wagon with the night quite dark because the moon burned out. He looked into the sky, but the buffalo were not there. But the Dancehall Girls were there and O'Ryan was just below them.

He rocked back and forth on the wagon seat holding tightly to himself and then the buffalo calf came out of the early morning fog and nuzzled him and he fell down against it on the ground and put his arm around its neck and sobbed, "Crissake."

The mule nickered to be unharnessed. But he paid no attention to her. She tossed her head and waited, sniffing the wind. The mule knew nothing of a trip out being the last. But she sensed the nights running out. She sensed the grass dying under the sun. She sensed that everything was older. She wondered about the Cheyenne ponies and if they still ran in the nights and where were the wild whoops she had known? And what was time?

five For about a month Rapaho still hunted in the hills with the mule pulling the wagon and the calf which would not go away trailing in the dust.

"Reckon you're the only calf that ever went buffalo huntin," he would tell it.

In the late part of September he left the hills and went down on the flat of the land to scout for new sign. But even the buffalo gnats were gone and grass was growing thick and blue where wallows had been.

"Kin they really all be dead?"

In October he moved back in the hills and set up his camp where it had been that first time, on the downgoing side of the hill where two cottonwoods half-stood half-leaned and there was a trickle of water that could hardly be called a stream. A few rocks.

"When the wind turns around, if they's any buffalo, they'll hafta come this way."

By days he sat on the hill and looked at the land around him and below him. It was turning red now that fall had come, and in some places browning. The sky came bluer than before. There were calico sunsets. There was not so much fog from the river below. There were a lot of clouds popping up over the western horizon. The sun was farther

51

off and sometimes hazey. A few late flowers which were the size of his thumbnail and were yellow bloomed. The dew stayed on longer in the mornings. The ground felt almost moist. A lot of bugs buzzed.

Sometimes an antelope would rush past below, jumping to one side then the other, cutting a winding trail which closed up again behind it. He would watch it out of sight, then sit for a long time waiting for something else to come along. There might be the rumble of mustang hoofs to the north and he would make out their dust cloud rising whitely against the sky. Then he would sigh and wait for something else to come along. Hawks, buzzards, eagles and other birds flapped over. And he would doze and wait for something else to come along.

But very little came along. The land was empty. Unless you count badgers, pocket gophers, kangaroo rats as something else. Rapaho did not.

Day after day the grass just stood in the sun, turning red, redder, reddest red, and finally brown, ready to fall down with the first winter snow. Here and there would be a boulder sticking up in the sun where the grass beside it had brittled and bent in some night wind. Off to the west was a cottonwood whose top was gone. To the north there was a blue streak that meant a tall bluff. To the east, behind him, down the range of hills there were five cottonwoods by the river. That was all he ever saw. That and the grass. Rippling a little in the low ground wind. Standing stiff and still, each blade of it catching the sun on all its sides. Breaking where it had long been dried by the hot winds. Once to the south it caught on fire after a storm of purple clouds that hung like rags and had red lightning in them. He had heard the thunder of the fire even in his sleep and woke to the grey smoke and rolled over to watch dark antelope shapes and coyote shapes leaping before it. But that was the only thing that happened that was different. Nothing came to mash down the grass. Nothing ate it. Nothing slept on it. So he just sat and watched it hoping . . . and it just stood and watched nothing and did not hope.

In late October he started looking toward the southwest. That's where the hunters, the hide men and the skinners would be coming from. If they came.

"They'll come."

That's where he'd see their specks and hear their yells, their guns shot off for the hell of it. If they came.

"Sure . . . they gotta come . . . they already bought their stores."

That's where he'd see their fires. If they came.

"But . . . they   ain't   comin."

Only a stray mirage ever came up out of the southwest. Nothing else.

A wagon went by on the trail below four-five times maybe. Dust blew up from somewhere that a settler was plowing. Men, sometimes just one, sometimes as many as five, rode by on horses in the same direction the wagon had gone. Once he thought he heard a train screaming to the northeast. One morning he saw a telegraph line glittering very far off, or so he thought. And there was some bobwire too, way to the east.

Nothing changed. Nothing went back to the way it had been. Nothing new came along either.

He knew at last there was not going to be any hunting. And he also knew that before the snow came on he would have to move out and go down to Santa Fe or somewhere else.

"Gotta make plans," he said.

But when he picked up a stick to draw maps from his

53

head, he just made curlicues with it in the dirt. When he tried to think, the flutes in his head drowned out the words. When he tried to sort over what he had left of his stores, he found himself just standing like the grass and staring toward where the Cheyenne drum still called his name. When he tried to choose between the four directions of a white man or the ten directions of an Injun, the moon would boom. Each night when he took off his jacket and hat and the eagle claw from his ear and the bracelets and rings and tucked them under the wagon seat, he'd say, "Tomorrow . . . I'll decide . . . and go." But each morning when he got up and put the jacket and hat and eagle claw and bracelets and rings back on and saw another monotonous day leaning there on the grass, he'd say, "Tomorrow . . . tomorrow for sure."

The calf and mule grew fat. The mule got lazy so that her lantern jaw seemed to sneer when she passed by the wagon and whisked her tail at it. The calf just played. Butted crickets. Charged grass when it tickled its nose. Tried to push over rocks. Wallowed in the trickle of water. Danced on the hills and the flat below, for sometimes the mule and calf would graze off together from the hills. Usually Rapaho would be able to see them and he would watch them with the Big Fifty laid across his lap in case a coyote jumped up in front of them and bared its teeth as coyotes did to scare the fragile antelopes and make them run and tire so they could be pulled down.

But nothing ever frightened them. Nothing stalked them. Nothing took out after them. They would graze farther and farther away and one morning when he woke, they'd be out of sight so that he would fret—for they were all he had to break the lonely boredom of another day—and he would say, "Well, Mr. Rapaho, we can't go away today without our mule and calf," and be relieved about the maps and stores and the directions, but worried about them. He'd fill his canteen at the trickle, slap on his hat, sling his gun over his shoulder and walk down onto the flat to search for them.

He always found them, though it tired him some, and they and he would be glad to see each other coming across the empty plain. Those nights when they came home again he'd lay out a feast of beans and bacon and flour balls, which they both liked, and grass he'd found which had a special look about it, and give them Taos Lightning from his hat, which they also liked. He'd talk to them and tell them stories as if they were human young'uns and sometimes sing them songs about foxes who went hunting and Promised Lands. The mule would stand off from him and roll her round brown eyes. But the calf would collapse beside him and cuddle its head against his legs. So they'd sit into the night with Rapaho crooning and talking, petting the calf and blowing on its fur that was coming in with a bluish cast and admiring its hoofs which were not brown or black but were some other color that he thought green.

"What friends I coulda had that I went and killed," he would say.

It was in there sometime that he decided he would not hunt anymore.

✳ When Jesse S. preached, everyone got the rousements. He would swagger up and down the bed of the wagon that had rattled them to Kaintuck. It was all saggy with one of its corners propped on a locust stump and its scarred tongue grown over with orange bittersweet. It was third or fourth handed already when they bought it down in Finncastle, Virginia the winter Jabal was nine. Jesse S. had kicked a wheel off it by accident—just poking at it to see its condition after they'd bogged in Paint Lick he kicked a wheel off it. The wheel had stayed where it fell and turned mossy with wild morning glory winding in and out among its spokes. Jesse S. had built their cabin hard by, saying if the Lord meant them to go farther, then He'd have made the wheel resist a mortal kick.

To the young'uns, who believed him, the wagon was a sacred thing, an altar of God, the place where Abraham laid Isaac down, the Ark that David danced before, and they were awed that it had fetched mortals such as them thru the foggy mountains with Jesse S.' rifle under the seat and them fighting in the wagon bed among the plunder of kettles, patchwork comforters, cornhusk pallets, and the bow legged rocking chair that had belonged to their grandma so long it looked like her, even in its bottom.

All the way up from Finncastle Jesse S. had preached from the wagon bed, toeing young'uns and dishes and puppies out of his way. He'd talked to long-hunters ranging by with their traps on their backs and their eyes black and fearsome. He'd talked to lone women with chickens racketing round them in the dust. He'd even talked to the babes and young'uns wrapped up in wild grape vines of games. Even the nights and mighty trees got a talking to when no human hailed their fire. But after they stopped by Paint Lick folks came by to be preached to. Jesse S. took it as a further sign from the Lord and was content to stay awhile, though his eyes were always turning after the black eyes of the long-hunters and their moccasins polishing the earth.

When Jesse S. got up to talk everybody would be quiet. The men would smoke the bitter Injun tobacco. The women would sew. The young'uns sat the stillest because their folks said to.

But as Jesse S. got on with it, his voice pitching and swooping, like a haggard on the hunt after food for her eaglets, the men began to let their pipes go cold and the women to snag their thread and the young'uns to listen for the pure pleasure of the Shawnee rhythm of his voice.

Amen.

Do you hear us talkin, Lord?

Yes, we are terrible sinners. Oh, Jesse S. it's true.

Jesse S. eyebatted them down, his tongue the sword of an avenging angel slashing at the host of the damned, turning on hickory spits down in hell. He began to rock back and forth and they rocked with him, their own bodies cradled in their own everlasting arms. Each face its own rock against the ages of sins. Each heart abiding unto itself.

57

But the moment of sweet understanding lasted only a moment.

Soon they lurched to their feet to reel like Jesse S. . . . The women catching the toes of their shoes in the hems of their linsey skirts and stepping the hems out, unmindful. The men dropping their pipes as their hands suddenly twitched open, unable to hold tight to anything. The young'uns hopping up because their elders did and because it was like a sacred frolic and they did blow the trumpets of their throats before the ark of God. (Hid there it is amongst the bittersweet . . . its horns worn down from being yoked mercifully mossed over . . . its poor tired wheels, the three it stands on, the one it don't, resting peacefully on the threshing floor of the Lord where the wind is the only flail.)

Soon they were saying words no man on earth could have put a meaning to. *Words from God,* they cried, *and Isaiah and Elijah,* and tossed their heads as if to churn from them the simple words of mortal men and let the heaven words pour in thru their glazing eyes. Blobs of sound came from their quivering lips, but they knew, *they knew* what they were saying and Oh, glory be to God on the highest and on earth peace to all men of good will because *they knew.*

The battle was at the gate now as some wrenched at their clothes and snatched off precious buttons to fling away in the purple leaf mould as evil things not tooled by the hand of God. The dear ornaments, the little locket the baby cut his tooth on, the shell comb their great grandma wore down in Georgia, the jet earrings their man had given them as his only wedding gift were cast away as the gibbering tongues commanded, for *No, I did not make these here devil's ornaments,* thus saith the Lord.

They danced on the hills. Among the black-eyed trees. Across the rock-toothed streams where Injuns hid. They danced till they fell down in the mud. Squealing in the mud. Digging their elbows in the mud. Leaving their bone and nose prints in the mud. And then they got themselves up and they danced some more out across the open spaces of the fields. In and out among the killed burned trees they had planted. Where the tamed crops stood to grow, they danced. Where the tamed crops trembled in the night air with their growing, with their white juice pushing into leaf and stem, with their buds rounding, with their corn going into milk, they danced. Where the tamed crops stood, guarded by day by the young'uns against the digging varmints and the hungry birds, but now only guarded by the silent scarecrows whisking their ghosty arms of dried grass against the wild people who had made them but whom they could not frighten, they danced. They danced them down, the tamed crops. Down into the ground. In their agony of religion they thought not about what they would harvest when harvest came.

(Sorrow of the morning. The little lockets gone, the shell combs lost, the jet earrings ground into the jet ground. The crops. Sorrow when they would cry inside as they walked the open fields and paused to touch with tenderness the tamed crops they had violated. Touched and propped and tried to make grow again. Touched and breathed against and whispered to and tried to make live again. Sorrow when the corn was killed and the gold buttons still lay hidden in the purple leaf mould.)

Repent, Jesse S. cried.
I do . . . Oh, I do.

59

Come to Christ.
I do . . . Oh, I do.

The night fires blossomed round them. The night stars flittered above them. Their feet went up to the moon. The night beasts watched from afar, yurring and growling in their thickets. The crickets hushed. The peepers crept back into the mud.

Repent, Jesse S. cried.
I do . . . Oh, I do.

The Shawnee warriors, painted and ready with battle axes, hid and watched. The Shawnees hid, seeing the evil spirit upon the white man. The Shawnee warriors, who watched, crept away with their bows cold against their sides and their quivers rattling full. They ran away from the shuffling mass and into the violet-scented deep black soft sighing woods, for they were afraid. The Shawnees who watched, they went back to their villages and told their lean war chiefs, and their fat tribal chiefs, and their witch-faced medicine men how the white men were overtaken by an evil spirit named Repent. And then for a long time the hunters were forced to stay in the villages so that the children choked on the dried corn of the last harvest and hungered for bloody meat because the hunters were afraid that the evil spirit called Repent was waiting for them, too, in the forest.

✳ Sometimes when Jesse S. got to preaching in the rhymes he fell down and got to foaming at the mouth. When he could raise himself from it he would gouge the young'uns with his eyes and shout, "Even Saul had a evil spirit fall upon him and hollered for David to sing a hymn and the Lord let down a cherubim from the brim of the rim of the dim dim dim . . ." and he would falter because he was out of rhyming words and that would make the fits come even worse so that their ma would get the chair and call them to help tie him down. That was why they kept grandma's rocker chair at all. It was also why the rockers were broken—from going over backward so much. And when their pa sat in it with his arms roped to its arms, they couldn't see the pale disc of the mother-of-pearl moon set in the back of it.

The young'uns got so when their pa seemed bad or like he might be heading for a tying-down fit, that when they came into the cabin the tips of their lashes sought out the moon on the back of the chair. If they could see it, he wasn't there. If they couldn't see it he was there. They never saw him. It was something strange, but they never saw him. They saw a lumpy sort of shadow, yet not a shadow but more a lack of light. In those times when the moon was dark and their ma didn't swing out the door for strangers, but stood broad in it and elbowed either side and lied, "No, Jesse S. ain't here . . . he's off a huntin . . ." and then turned back to look at him and wonder where and what he hunted—in those times the young'uns were quick to see where the chair stood from the fire and were its four feet and two uneven rockers quiet on the floor or were there two other feet shoving and pushing it around the cabin—in those times they worried about the chair. They had no other.

Once the chair had fallen in the fire when their pa had kicked it over even though his boots had been hidden from him and burrs spread over the floor. Deep down in the woods they heard him, a sound neither wolf nor wind, said to each other, *The moon.*

Jabal got burned all the way to one shoulder that time, and the girl got her knees burned, and another boy, a neighbor boy, his hand. Only his hand, for he saw the man tied to the chair and he held back, stood back with his toes gripping the front edge of the hearthstone and only put his hand out at the very last.

The fits would taper off. They said he was no longer bad. He would break loose slyly and creep up the loft ladder to where the young'uns slept. And they would stir, knowing his presence. Not knowing from a sound or smell. But knowing from the feel of fear which preceded him up the ladder like a dark ghost never seen but often touched. Then they would hear him breathing. They would turn their eyes to the loft hole where the light was yellow from the fire below and the idea that hell was a cabin beneath a loft was very strong in their minds. They would say to themselves, *It ain't him breathin—it's only the wind.* And they would reach out cold hands to each other in the dark.

✳ "A purty night, boy. Hear that wind a rollin round."

And Jabal heard it as they rushed past it, his pa's boots kicking at the dark that clung in the thickets, his pa's hand tight on his arm just above the elbow. He wanted to say, *It hurts,* but chewed his tongue quiet because to say *It hurts* would not help. Would only mean a harder push. Would only mean a tighter thumb screwed into his neck. His pa's hands were printed on his body on the windy nights that made him restless.

Under the sycamore they stopped.

"Sit down, boy," his father would say. And he would sit, trying to be small and another blob of dark. Trying not to show so that his pa would forget him. He never did forget him, but always Jabal hoped . . .

The wind rose. Only it didn't sound so much like wind there under the sycamore. It sounded more like people sighing, a lot of people sighing together and trying to get their breath again after crying, and sometimes there was one who made a gaspy sound that was not a scream nor sob, but was like the sound the baby made when their ma's hands were cold. His pa's voice was muffled by the wind so that he had to listen hard, for his pa would ask him questions about what he had said. It was harder to hear above the wind because he didn't want to hear, to answer, to be there under the sycamore. The wind would drop, he'd hear part of a word, strain for the rest, but the wind would rise again and carry the word on past him till so many words were gone off into the night that he would begin to shake and grow still smaller because it was no use to try to hear above the wind and soon he would have to answer and when he couldn't there would be that thumb gouged in his neck for not listening as he should. It seemed to him that the windy nights were the darkest. Also the wettest around the eyes. The most painful. And he'd lean forward a little and try, really try to hear, with his mouth open a little and his eyes wide and his fists tight. But there was only the see-sawing sound of a world blowing past him and the touch of fear in the palms of his hands which made them tickle.

"I tell you, Jabal, because you're the oldest and you orter understan. I was the oldest too. But no one ever took me out from my brothers and my sisters and set me under a tree and talked to me like this. My pa . . . he didn't care about me. But I care about you, boy, and that's why I always single you out from the others. You and me, Jabal, we're lots alike. Your ma," a sneer, "she ain't much. A woman. Sweeps out the cabin. Has babies. Bout all you kin say. Your brothers and sisters . . . not much there either. Weak and skinny and no sense. But you're like your old pa. You got sense. I kin talk to you cause I know you understan."

But understand what? What, pa? What? What?

". . . Jabal, did I ever show you the way *my* folks beat *me?*"

The thumb went in deeper and he knew the other hand was jerking down his pa's breeches, then he had to stare thru the dark at the backs of his pa's legs where the deep scars were and he had to touch them . . .

"Run your hands over em, Jabal. Feel em. They're like pits, by God."

And the thumb screwing hand would let go long enough to pull Jabal's thin fingers down hard against the pits which were always hot as though they still burned with pain and blood.

It always started out like this, but then it got onto other things. If there was a moon it would come and go so that sometimes there'd be a bit of light and Jabal would see the man across from him thru the matted stick-tights that hung over his right eye. He would stare at the thong which pulled his pa's shirt together at the neck. He would watch the sway of the feather fastened to the end of the thong. *I kin always tell what the weather's goin to be by this here feather . . . if it's damp at night, 'twon't rain tomorrow.*

"Your feather's wet," he whispered, hoping to turn the talk onto other things, but his pa didn't hear, and he got up the courage to whisper it again, this time a little louder, and he leaned forward and his pa saw his mouth move and said back, "What?" "I said your —" And the wind took care of the rest of it, and he was sorry he'd said anything because now he had to say it loud enough to hear and the wind was roaring even thru his head and his pa's face was dark and the thumb tighter and "What?" "Feather's wet." It came out in a shout and his pa leaned back abruptly and felt the feather and studied it and the light that was his eyes went out for a moment being shined down on the feather, and Jabal was afraid for fear it really wasn't wet but had only looked it . . . .

65

But it is dripping, pa. He was sure he saw it dripping from the sycamore above. Maybe it was the spittle of locusts that dripped from above. Maybe it was dew. Maybe it was something from his pa's beard, something run down like soup, and he smelled for his pa's breath but only picked up the smell of burned johnnycake made on the maple johnnycake board lugged from where ma and pa called home and *what was home?* And he blurted out, "Yes," because he hadn't been thinking or listening and he was afraid his pa had said something he should answer to and yes was the safest and he was so sleepy and he wished—oh, how he wished. . . .

"And how come you to run aroun all day with them green sticky-tights over your eye like some bush boy . . . like some Shawnee . . . like you never knowed no better and how do that look for a preacher's son?"

"Dunno, pa." And he shoved the stick-tights back and caught them as if to pull them loose, and let go slowly as if they fought, then dropped his hand and let them fall back before his eye because he felt safer with something there and as if he were partly hidden.

". . . four days ago. And I was gonna fetch you back one of Birdie Kamper's hound-that's-such-a-good-hunter's pups. In fact, I did fetch one back, but when I come in the cabin with it your ma says, 'He's been such a bad boy, hangin round out in the woods with that crazy old hunter and not fetchin warter right off when I asked him and haulin his baby sister around when he shoulda been cuttin wood and I ast him to go out and ketch us somethin to eat and he never went and says he don't kill nothin and I says "You better learn!" and I give him a good whompin but it don't do no good . . .' So when she tells me all that,

I just throwed that pup back up over my shoulder and back I lugged him . . ."

Tears started up in Jabal's eyes because he believed it. He believed it all.

". . . ain't mean to you . . . oldest boy . . . like me . . . good and smart. . . ."

And then his pa sounded like he was crying, too, and Jabal held his own neck stiff and shook inside and, my God, how could he have sinned so much and never even seen it and why didn't his pa beat him? And he went down on his knees in the weeds with his head in his pa's lap and he had wanted that puppy forever and prayed hard for it and sneaked round eying the hound and wondering when she going to drop them and it had even been in the cabin and seen the fire and been so happy to have a home and so eager to meet him and now it was gone back to its ma who had thought it was bad and punished it already and said, Why did they bring you back, less you was bad? What would become of that little puppy that had been hanging over his pa's arm just a few hours back? Whatever would become of it without him who would have been so good to it?

"You know I fetched it fer you, don't you?"

"Yes, pa."

"And ain't you sorry now you was bad to your ma and didn't get the pup?"

"Yes, pa."

"And ain't you shamed?"

"Yes, pa."

"And wouldna you liked to of had it?"

"Yes, pa."

"And would you like fer me to go back and fetch it again?"

"Yes, pa."

His eyes flared up with hope and he tried to hold his lashes low because he knew how his eyes would give him away and he pulled the stick-tights a little lower because he didn't want his pa to see the hope so bright that it was like full moonlight, but oh, God, if he would only fetch it back for him, he'd be so good, he'd promise anything—his own puppy to love and go off with him and they could wiggle thru the weeds together like Injuns and they could fish together and they could even stay out nights together and sleep in the woods when the wind was sobbing and his pa was breaking loose from the tying-down fit and his pa would reach and feel for him in the loft but he'd be gone and safe with his puppy. . . .

"And have you got a name picked out fer it in your head?"

"Yes, pa."

"What is it?"

"Darvish."

"That's a funny name fer a hound dog. Where'd you ever hear it?"

"I never. I made it up."

"Like you made up the story about forgettin about the warter bucket and chasin a snake instead cause you thought it was poisonous and might hurt your ma?"

The wind stood up again and his shoulders fell and why hadn't his pa said anything more about the puppy and when were they going to get back to that and how could a thumb hurt so much and was that locusts' spittle after all?

"Yes, pa."

It was true about the snake and him chasing it, but no one would ever believe him. It was both wrong to tell the truth and to lie because nobody ever believed either one. Whatever he said or did it was wrong and that was what the wind knew that made it go *Hreeee* in the sycamore. Now his father wasn't only breathing in his mouth, but spittle from his lips was flying against Jabal's face and he felt dirty and wanted to wipe it off quick and wanted to pull back because the thumb was dug so hard that a blood vein was knotted up against it and the sycamore was starting to go around.

"Liar. Liar and a bad boy . . . that's all you ever was and all you ever will be. Lyin and lazyin and not fetchin the warter when you was told and not killin no food and what about your little sister . . . she's got to eat too. Your ma and me and the others you don't care about . . . we kin die . . . but your little sister you care about and whyn't you fetch some food fer her?"

Jabal bit his lips together. I will not answer him, he swore to the wind with his eyes down, because she eats from ma and she don't eat dead things and he knows it and he knows I know, so why is he askin me such a mean thing and yes, I'd kill for her . . . even him for her . . . God forgive me and watch over those who trespass against Thee and all the days of my life forever I shall stand on the hill of the Lord in the valley of the shadow of death where I fear no evil . . . amen.

The other thumb caught him below the shortribs now and he began to shiver with his eyes squeezed tight because if the puppy were his it would not let his pa hurt him like this—it would jump and yap and bite the thumbs that gouged so hard—but then the puppy was kicked and rolled over in the dark fern and it cried and would never be well again but always drag a crooked leg and favor a hurt deep inside and soon die.

69

"You want the pup, don't you now?"

It would love him and try to protect him and it would die.

"You want it!"

"No, pa."

They would not sacrifice his Isaac. He would not lay him on an altar and let him be burned for his own sake and yea though I walk in the valley of the shadow of death I will not take my puppy with me.

The thumbs let him go.

"Ongrateful! I try to . . . sayin you want a pup . . . try to fetch . . . do my best . . . God knows . . . Could a been like Juniper's boy . . . hunts and fetches warter . . . more than he's ast . . . sets and sings purty songs . . . sing me a song . . . come on, singy-song me a song."

Jabal held on tight to the rocking earth with his skin all drawn in bumps and he felt a shaking inside like something was going to burst and lots of black powder pour out and he wouldn't be there anymore but all apart in pieces and that made him shake some more because if you could fly all apart in pieces what happened to you then because he didn't think anyone would even look for any of the pieces to bury and some of them would probably stick up in the top of the sycamore and lots of them would be scattered down under the fern and the berry bushes where he used to like to go when he was young——

" . . . said sing to me, damn your hide!"

He pushed back and saw his pa had taken out his long knife that he always kept at his belt and he was leaning on it and kind of rocking like he was in the rocker when it still had rockers. He must not blow apart and leave only black powder, for who would look after his sister, frail and weak, and the thumbs would kill her if they ever touched her and the whack on the head with their ma's johnnycake board would kill her too and he must not become pieces and powder.

"*The fox went out on a wintery night*
And he p-p-prayed for the m-m-moon to give him
    light——"

"Quit that stutterin."

"*For he'd m-m-many a mile to go that night*
Before he reached th-th-th town-o."

At his feet he thought he heard the whimpering of the little puppy that would never be his.

six

Hutch woke with the sun's yellow smoke in his eyes and the settler's grey wind in his mouth.

God, but it's hot.

The wind wasn't moving much. Maybe up in the mountains, west, way west and up in the mountains where it was always cool and streams came out of snow, the wind was moving. But here it mostly stood head down in the southwestern corner of the world, sweating like a horse worked hard before a dull-bitted plow.

He ran his tongue around inside the dryness of his mouth and slept again a moment and dreamed a tall woman came fetching water in a green peeled gourd. She was a Shawnee woman and wore fresh water pearls around her wrists. The water she gave him tasted like sweet cold wine. Blackberry wine. As he drank it he saw beyond her shoulder the spring where it welled up. A dark spring with thick ferns tall as a man and so deep a green they were almost black. There was blue cabin smoke drifting out over the spring and he hallooed the cabin, choked on the water, and woke again. Woke to the smoky sun and the heat. Woke to the panting air where nothing stirred. Woke to the heat of the ground beneath him. Even the ground, it was hot. When he pressed his calloused hands down against it seeking some cool left behind by the night, there was the heat curling up under his snaggy fingernails and burning the tender skin which remained white underneath the nail.

He sniffed the air then. It was going to be a real bad one. A real dog days August one. A scorcher. Though it was October.

Hey, Jesse S., it's going to be a real scorcher, ain't it?

And he went back that quick to when he was a boy in Kaintuck and July and the Fourth of it. It was always a scorcher back there, with the ragged-headed mountains and the ragged-headed trees shutting out the air.

How the sweat darkened the fringe of the mens' leggings as they moccasined thru the tanglement of forest to the bony settlement where the ground was black and mossy and blue around the knees with shafts of feathery chickory. Their matted hair, tied back with strings of bark and whang, flickered across their swinging shoulders, long threads of it sometimes catching in a haw tree to blow like a shattered spider web. Their women gathered heavy skirts to run behind them, bobbling like wild turkeys, big gourds of food in their ropey arms and babes slung from shawls in the Injun way. The young'uns coming on their own, stitched together with their fingers, and sometimes one breaking away and leaving two hands on either side working to grab it back while it ran off to stand among the fearsome shadows of the trail and scare itself a moment with the sighing of the lonesome wilderness.

Then the settlement of four grey cabins and a fifth that was new and still sprouted leaves leaped up before them where there was sky to see and even sun. And all the men shot off their squirrel guns. Shrieked like Shawnees dripping paint. Pried the black wet bung from a barrel of raw-gutted whiskey just freighted down from the Ohio. Drank while chewing johnnycake and fried turkey. Roared and curtsied a step or two to Jesse S.' fiddle while night came down and the stars popped out for the young'uns to sort from the green fireflies.

Hey, Preacher Jesse S. . . . give us a speech . . . a reg'lar Fourth of July talkin to . . .

And Jesse S., Hutch's pa, jumped up on the woodpile against Edsell's Store and braced himself against the purple and red sign——THIS IS A STORE——and gave them a speech to pound their feet to.

. . . and if that ain't true, you ask ol Livvy there . . . he fit the Rev'lution . . . yessir, he fit the Rev'lution. Step up here, Livvy. Don't be backward like my boys. Step up and tell em how you fit the Rev'lution and winned some whole battles by your ownself and winned, by God. Winned.

And then Jesse S. turned back to the crowd of sweat-shined men and women squatting on the moss and he began to beat his hands together like he heard a tune played somewhere that no one else could hear.

He stood like a rock at Manassus,
(Quit leanin gainst me, Livvy.)
Like a rock at Manassus,
While the Yankees howled in the grasses,
(Watch out, Livvy . . . you're gonna fetch down the sign if you don't quit haulin on it. Stand up by your ownself!)
Twixt Manassus and Parnassus——
(Whereat's Parnassus, Jesse S.?)
Parnassus . . . while them Yankees run over the ground like maple molasses . . . and yea Lord, but shorely to God he did fight and winned!

Hutch sighed, coming back from Kaintuck so quick, called back by the sun and wind.

A right good time was had by all, he remembered. A downright good whoopin, hollerin, hell-raisin, panther-spittin, bear-cussin time!

He sighed again. This was not Kaintuck and he was not a boy but an old man and he was going to have to lug water to the sad bean plants in the back patch because it was a scorcher.

He might have to walk a mile upstream to get to where the deep pool always gave up scooping water and there were small delicate ferns the sun didn't know about under the overhanging bank and water bugs lacing up and down and water snakes curling by the crooked dam he'd stacked out of dead cottonwoods and half a day's sweat.

What a feller orter do, he thought, is either move the dam down or the field up.

He opened his eyes and closed them quick again.

It's too far to lug water down and too far to lug a hoe up.

He sighed. The field would stay where it was and the dam where it was for likely he wouldn't have to worry after either give another year or two.

How long can a old man live?

He reached up to pull his broad floppy hat down over his eyes and maybe sleep again. But the hat was gone. Rolled off down the hill by the last wind that passed that way, he reckoned. He reached out for the hat with his eyes still shut and touched its faded yellowness, felt its tatterdiness.

Need a new hat, he thought, and clamped the old one on his face. What a feller orter do . . . other hand . . . been thru a lot, this one. Days. Nights. Blizzards. Summers. Likely, it'll last me.

His raggedy hair lying across his chest was hot and in some places had snugged in under his shirt where it stung his skin with its edges. Now he reached out and lifted the

75

hair and fanned it back and forth across his chest to cool him some. Sometimes he wore his hair cut short, chopped off with his cabin knife. But then when he wasn't looking, it got long again and here it was smothering him.

Seems like I always go and cut it toward winter. He chewed on his lips. And then when summer comes, I forget it again. Got to cut it, he told himself, and went on fanning it across his face.

He clawed his blue shirt open and lay there with the sun beating on him. His clothes were the rough ragged things the frontier fetched up to him. But he had little interest in what he wore now that he was older. *Oldish* an old man would have called him. *Real staggering doggoned old* a young man would have said. By his own reckoning he was somewhere around sixty . . . maybe seventy . . . a little before . . . a little behind.

For a long time he had kept count of it, but he had let it slip. There was no reason to keep count. There was no one *to care how old he got. So you're sixty . . . I don't feel so good myself, so what?* That's what a drover had said to him one time when he'd gone into Three Trails on what he thought to be his birthday and was set to celebrate. So that's how it was that the end paper in the Bible was missing a lot of year-marks. Some before the drover had smarted off to him and some after. Anyway, little ever happened that was worth making a mark to remember it by, and then a lot of years slipped past him here and there what with him being busy with mending fences and adding onto the house and watering the bean plants and all. . . .

The day wore on. The sun climbed higher. The buffalo bushes began to sag against his side. He shoved them, but still they fell against him. Things flew by and left their shadows on his eyelids. "Eagle," he said once. The ground shook as a herd of something passed below his hill. "Ante-

lope," he said, "no . . . ponies." Dust came drifting on the
still air and he wiped his hand across his nose and knew that
down a way Scoggins was working his field. Like a slave,
he thought. That's all that feller is to that old patch . . . just
a slave. If the good Lord means em to grow, they'll grow
and ain't no sense in stirrin round and worryin em.

Cool made him open his eyes. Cool on his skin that made
it suddenly chill. Cool running its taste over his mouth.

Ahhhhhhhhhh.

Big dark clouds were coming up the horizon now shutting out the sun. Wet clouds, all feather edged. They built
and puffed like the horizon was a hard pull. But still they
came with the sun on their backs not slowing them down.
Soon he could smell the wet on their air. It was like leaning
over the horsetrough on a hot day with his head way down
deep in the stone damp where snails clung in the dark and
spider bugs silked along. The horsetrough smelled like
earth because it came from earth. And it smelled like violets
too. To him it smelled like violets. To him the violet smell
was all the things of earth alive and dead. Lush. Black.
Green. Frail budding sickly white that moved down below
the top of the ground where the violets and grassroots
touch. And it made him think about Kaintuck again where
there were trees all thick and tender standing strong like
men walking with no burdens on their backs.

Not like out here where men crawled along after plows
and wagons that shattered against hidden rocks. Where
men dragged after the quick-footed game that ever outran
them. Where men tossed clothes, trunks, chairs, clocks,
dishes out of the pitching Conestogas under sail when they
were eying the mountains to the west and the thinning oxen
which chewed their cuds slower now that the green woods
were lost to them forever.

Out here a man's back just purely broke under the sky.

77

Just it was too heavy a burden, worse than anything carried by a Conestoga, and a man never got to stand up straight and walk like the big trees of Kaintuck because the sky threatened him and he was afraid. Always talking to it. Begging it to give him lots of rain, but please no hail. Begging it for sun in the proper time. Begging it to hold back the wind from his tender corn. And begging it And please don't let me die . . . don't go and kill me . . . I got too many young'uns and anyway I'm scared to die. Hell might be worse. And then, Forgive that last dear God because I don't know what I'm sayin most the time I'm so tired and sun-struck.

He pulled his knees up to his chin and tried to let the wet air that was coming cool his backsides some. He pulled some sprigs of buffalo grass down over his eyes and stared out thru it where an ant waved its head back at him.

"That's why I lived to be so old," he said, "cause I don't leap up and fight no sky nor nothin else."

Like the time that rancher had cut his bobwire fence that it took him three crops to pay for. And he had just stood there, frazzledy hat in hand and his grimy head tilted back to look at the sky like what else could the rancher do. And he said, *Yessir . . . I shouldna put it up.* And all the time he was thinking, Took me three crops to pay for it and now it's gone. Three crops and I never got any good out'n it cept seein it shine two days in the sun and one night in the moon. It was shorely purty but I only got that little tiny bit of use out'n it. But then . . . shouldna put it up. He had his right to cut it cause it coulda hurt his cattle if they rubbed against it, and I can always put up scarecrows and plant my bean field to the north where the sun ain't so good but they is a wooden fence and that's what I shoulda done first place and it's my own dadblamed fault I done throwed away the money of three crops. And Hutch had felt as sorry as the next man when the rancher turned up dead and he had joined the posse to track the man that killed him. We never found him, but I did my part and helped to lug the coffin and I give the widder a pretty shawl.

And there was that time the trail boss of some Texas herd had camped right at the ford where Hutch went for all his water before he built the dam. And he hadn't said to the trail boss, *Get off'n my ford.* No, he'd walked three miles to get to scooping water with the wooden yoke cutting his bony shoulders and the buckets slamming against his bony knees. And he had sneaked out before daylight to do it, afraid the trail boss might not want him to take any water from the stream. But it was his own stream. It was his claim they were camped on and he had the papers that said it was his and he thought of maybe taking them down to the trail boss and saying real soft, *Now, maybe you don't know . . . but this is my own stream and while I don't care if you fellers drawn some water from it, I wonder could you move down a mite from the ford cause I've got some awful sick corn . . . a powerful dry spell . . . corn has gotta pay this year counta losin three crops on the bobwire last year. . . .* But he had only gone on walking the three miles and sloshing half the water out no matter how ginger-footed he went, and they had camped right on and he had never said, *Go away.* And the next year he'd let the same trail boss camp at his ford again and had been real sad when the trail boss was found drowned after drinking a considerable amount of whiskey and he had led the prayer and buried the trail boss in his dead corn field.

And ten years ago when the Kiowas attacked that wagon train and he'd seen it all from the hill where he was gathering bones to sell at the freight yard at Three Trails, he had only run and hidden. He had run home and taken the mule and chickens in the house, shuttered the glassless windows, barred the door, and then hid in the dugout in the dark where the damp made his mouth water for sweet potatoes and squirrel like when he was a boy. While the Kiowas were yelping and killing down below his hill, he had stood down there in the hole in the ground and thought about sweet potatoes and squirrel. And he had been ashamed and read the Bible some. But what else could he do? If he got killed who would look after the mule and his chickens and his little house? And who would go to the fort each year to see if Dittany had come back? And who would fetch her home and look after her and call her sister, keep the curious away so they wouldn't ask what it was like to be an almost life-long captive of the Sye-ox. The house, the mule, everything he did and worked for was for Dittany when she came home.

He had built the house backed up to a low hill that sheltered it. Each spring, when the wind turned around and began to blow from the south and the snow went off and the spring rains fell, he could see the hill had crept down on his house some more. For three years now the hill had been even with the roof of his house. And now when the sod roof sprouted and put up tender grass and scarlet poppies the mule went onto the roof to graze. Sometimes in the night he would hear it stomping up above him, chomping at the sweet grass with its long teeth. Sometimes it stomped a little too hard and dirt sifted down thru the old wooden framework of the ceiling to fall over his cup and bowl. But he didn't mind. The mule needed the tender grass and scarlet poppies. And the dirt that fell finally got walked into the floor and he could always blow out his cup and bowl.

The small barn where the mule and chickens lived was hidden by the hill too, and the only thing a stranger would see from the ragged line of higher hills that faced the house

80

would be the few cottonwoods bending to the wind and the line of buffalo bushes snorting up and down the stream. Even his chimney didn't stick up like a trail mark because it came up underneath the cottonwood that had blown from the low hill and the smoke wound up thru the branches like a cottonwood's fine grey mass of leaves shivering in the sun.

It was still with the stillness of a world apart down in his hollow. But sometimes in the winter the lean ribbed coyotes loped over his roof, sniffing the dried meat that hung just beneath and tearing at the sod with ice crusted claws. But the sod was frozen, and they always went on, barking that the meat couldn't be gotten and barking that the hunt was still on and barking out a few coyote cuss words, he thought.

He was always sorry that he couldn't feed them and he didn't know, at such times, whether he hoped his little pet was among them or not. He hated to think of it going hungry and having to run on its delicate legs with the pack. And yet he hated to think of it as dead.

But if it's with the others, he'd tell himself, they'll look out for it, it bein such a little feller and all and brought up without no ma nor pa . . . just me . . . a man that didn't know how to teach it much.

He had raised his coyote pup, sucking it on a rag wet with milk fetched from the neighbor every day. But it had turned wild in the end. It had been tamed at first and jumped up in his arms when he came home and flickered his face with its tongue and wagged its tail like a dog. But in the end it had turned wild. Stalked the chickens. Dug for prairie dogs. And it seemed to forget more and more to jump up in his arms. And then one morning it was gone.

He had called and called it. Tried trailing it. Even rid-

81

den the mule out to hunt it. But he had never found it. Yet, sometimes in the night he thought he heard it out on the hills scaring the sky with its lonesome calls.

At first he used to light his pipe and go outside and listen and feel comforted, and he thought it was talking to him and telling him how it was free and he was not to worry for it was well and happy, though it missed him some. He would smile way down deep inside where no one could see. And he would talk back to it under his breath and be certain that it heard and understood him way out there. Then it seemed like it howled farther and farther away and he got to climbing the rough-faced hills and calling it the way one coyote calls another. He got so he howled real good. So good that one night his neighbor, the neighbor with the cow, took a shot at him taking him for a Pawnee scout making like a coyote. After that, he didn't howl like a coyote anymore.

Often when the weather let up and the mustangs started drifting north they crossed his roof and he'd lie and listen to them snorting and pawing and whickering as they ran out into the hills. Often he heard jackrabbits arcing over the roof and then there were other small feet that went across that were there winter or summer. Prairie dog, mouse and lizard. He liked the feet on the roof. It made him feel less lonesome.

Inside the house he had furniture better than most folks had. Better than any he'd ever seen. Better than anything in Three Trails Hotel. The few people who'd ever been in his house showed with their eyes how grand it was and asked, *Whereat did you fetch it from . . . St. Looey?* And he'd only nodded and looked shy and like it didn't amount to that much. He hadn't the heart to tell them when they thought he was rich enough to buy it, that he had only stumbled on it up north where the old Lander Trail took off from the Mormon Trail and Scotts Bluff stood up sad.

There was a place up there where folks heading west often threw off what they couldn't bear to part with but couldn't bear to lug any farther. He called it the Conestoga Graveyard, and he'd found the velvet chairs first, their worn green backs like butterfly wings in the sun. He'd touched their softness and felt the rich round wood and he'd lifted them gentle onto the wagon. And since that time twice or more a year he hitched up the mule and made the long trip up to Scotts Bluff to see what else the Graveyard had.

He considered it God's blessing on him, for he was so poor he could never have bought that first chair. And he thought that because he was old and had had so little and had tried to live a good and honest life that God had at last led him to the Conestoga Graveyard and pointed it out to him as much as to say, *There . . . it's all your'n because I feel sorry for you and I've had my eye on you for a long long time.*

In the corner under the shelf where stood his shaving mug, seldom used, was a claw-footed table of some dark wood with a fine feathery plume tracing thru it. Beneath the two windows that looked to the south and opened and closed with shutters from inside, was a chest all carved with grapevines and inside filled with men's and women's clothes. The chest was handcarved, he thought as he ran his worn fingers over the knobbiness of the rich grapes and the twistiness of the slender vines. He always wondered who it was had carved it and had finally come to throw it away.

It had a man's name on it, M. Gruber. And he had always hoped to meet M. Gruber and to see what he looked like in the face. Yet, he hoped not to meet him too, for then he would be obliged to give back the chest which said

M. Gruber and which maybe M. Gruber was awful sorry
he'd parted with, and he imagined him sitting somewhere
by a mountain campfire with his head in his hands and saying, *I wisht I had it back . . . I made it with my own two
hands and it was the only thing I ever made and I wisht I
had it back.* And he imagined M. Gruber turning back. In
hunger and thirst and thru winter blizzards and summer
heat M. Gruber went back toward the chest, and behind
him were his young'uns and his woman left to worry where
he was. And then M. Gruber got to the Graveyard, and the
chest was gone. How the look on his face turned a man inside out, how tight, like he was dying. When Hutch
thought about it that way, almost he hitched the mule to
take the chest back and leave it. But in the end he didn't.
But the next time he went north to Scotts Bluff, he left a
note on a forked stick . . . I GOT YOUR CHEST. JABAL HUTCH-
INSON. WEST OF THREE TRAILS. DESCRAB AND CLAIME.

It was the best he could do, and just writing the note had
delayed him one day, for he couldn't write enough to brag
about but only enough to manage a simple word or two.

By the door stood some bedsprings. He'd tried to sleep
on them at first, but kept getting caught in their wiryness
and after he bent his finger in their coils he gave it up and
stood them on end by the door. There he hung his clothes
and rifle and hat. It was amazing how nice they were to
keep a place tidied up. On the back wall of the cabin, the
wall with no windows because that was where the hill was
and ants went in and out, he had tacked some cloth. He
had meant to make a curtain, and though he threaded a
needle specially bought for the purpose and stitched and
pulled it never looked like a curtain. Finally he just sort of
tacked it there and its blue calico print had swagged and
stiffened with dust thru the years.

Candle molds, for which he had no use, stood by the fire-place and he dropped into them all the things his pockets yielded up after he had been outdoors—small pebbles that caught his eye, tiny butterfly wings, dead bugs he wondered about, Injun beads. Above the fireplace were stacked the books he couldn't quite read, and to one side of the hearth there were three wooden chairs, one with arms. Around the walls leaned lithographs of other places and one was of a waterfall. When it was hot sometimes he closed the door and darkened the cabin with the shutters and sat in front of the waterfall and pretended he was there and soon he'd hear it roaring down the rocks and feel the spray tickling his nose and smell the sweet coolness of where the water came from.

In the middle of the room stood his prize from the Graveyard. He ate off of it every night after spreading a piece of calico on top. He ate from it with great care and reverence and never let a drop of water or a crumb of bread drop on its gleaming black finish that was inlaid all over with tiny ivory lace and mother-of-pearl.

It was a harpsichord.

He wished he could play it better. It was such a pure comfort to sit down to it and touch the keys and hear the notes of music lift into the air light as birds and float out thru his door over the wild land. It sure beat Cheyenne drums, which a man didn't hear anymore. Also Kiowa whistles, which were also scarce. Also Blackfoot rattles, which were only a remembered sound. They had been all right as long as there was nothing else. But when they had gone away, the Cheyenne and Kiowa to reservations and the Blackfoot just home, the Lord had seen how he missed some human sound that was akin to music so He had sent him a harpsichord.

One time when he was at Three Trails and right after he got the precious thing, he had stood in the Lucky Lady Saloon right behind the piano player and watched how fast his fingers went up and down on the keys. Then he'd kicked the mule all the way home, hurrying to get there before the notes and how you made them went out of his head. But it didn't come out the same. It was awful. He did manage, after a good many trips to the saloon, to bang out a sort of *Wabash Cannonball* and also *Gerry Owen*, which became quite popular after Custer was massacred. But that was about all he did manage. And though he'd gone back to the saloon and watched some more, he finally quit because he didn't know a soul in there and the people who did speak to him always wanted to play cards or to buy them a drink and he really couldn't afford to spend a nickel here and a nickel there and it was plain it wasn't meant for you to go without spending.

Now he yawned and looked back up at the sun. It was hotter than it had been. The wet clouds had slid down the other side of the sky.

He got to his feet, the battered hat sideways on his head, shading only one grey eye. He stuck his thumbs in the waist of his pants where the cord was tied tight and looked down on the cottonwoods and buffalo bushes. He looked at the sun falling on his land. On his stream. On his bean plants.

Them dern bean plants . . . water . . .

He swung, started glumly down the hill, then he remembered something else. This was the Sabbath. Yessir, Sunday. He smiled then. No lugging water today. The bean plants were on their own and good luck to you, I hope you hold out till tomorry. He was going to church, going to give the preacher another try.

"Fair is fair," he said.

The preacher down at Three Trails was nothing like his pa had been. Hutch doubted that the man was really a preacher. He came into the church very quiet like the wind was pushing him or he wouldn't have come in at all. And he stood very quiet, like he hoped no one would notice him, and he spoke very quiet so that sometimes you could say he was whispering. He spoke about being meek and accepting things and inheriting the earth, though from whom he never said, and how it was better to have no pride. Hutch thought he was not much as a preacher. He never accused the congregation of being sinners. He never aimed his finger at them and told how hot and miserable was hell. He never——

"Once he did raise his voice," he said aloud. "That time the dog came in and peed all down the bench. And another time he waved one hand a little, back when there was Injun trouble . . . but it could be his hand was shakin out of fear. But that was years and years ago. Still, he showed some promise then . . . and I ain't give up hope for him yet."

Inside the cabin it was dark after the light of the sun. But in a minute his eyes got used to the dark and he went to stand before the gilt-framed mirror which was cracked in three different places so that his image sort of wandered up and down thru it.

Hell, but I'm dirty.

So he turned around and poured some water out of the bucket by the door and washed in spots here and there. In M. Gruber's trunk he found M. Gruber's good blue suit. The coat was too short in the sleeves but not too tight and it fastened with all its buttons. The trousers were just a little short and baggy and his boots were dusty. He poured some water on them and then stood in the sun to let them dry. He fastened the shirt collar with *the* collar button and it found too, glittering bluely in the dust beneath Scotts Bluff. Then he stood before the mirror again.

Dern hair.

He got most of the snags out of it with the fork, and he rummaged in the trunk till he found a flat black hat that looked fitting. Outside the door he paused and picked a yellow flower and fastened it to his lapel with a thorn.

But when he went to get the mule, it had strayed, and though he yelled for it all over the place, it didn't come.

Tarnal, he thought, and walked carefully back up the hill, stepping wide to avoid the dusty patches and stopping ever so often to brush off the bottoms of his pants. He unfastened the collar too, and dropped the button gently in an inside pocket of M. Gruber's suit. But then he went slower because he was worried about the button and ever so often he would have to stop and poke his bony fingers into the pocket and pry around till he was sure it was still there.

"Only one I got," he said, "don't know when I'd ever find another."

He went on tracking the mule and calling. Then he saw it grazing over the brow of the third hill and he started to yell at it to come home quick so it would know he was mad and hurry. But then beyond it he saw something else. A wagon, a hunter's wagon, old and creaky looking and busted here and there with some feathers tied to its wheels and Injun signs painted on its side. He squatted down behind a boulder and thought.

Rapaho.

He reached into his pocket and felt for the collar button

again. Then he looked over the boulder again. But it was still there, the wagon.

Yessir, that's who . . . that ornery cuss the bounty hunter asked bout . . . left me the poster . . . said he'd share some with me . . . shoot, I knowed who it was . . . but he ain't never bothered me . . . still, I kinda rather he didn't camp up here so close.

He fingered the button and watched it shining in the sun.

Bet that bounty hunter lied . . . shoot, he ain't never even come down and tried to steal a chicken. Maybe he was sorry for what he done . . . and maybe he's just like me . . . old and tired. But, don't wanta rile him none. Don't wanta go into his camp makin a lot of noise about the mule. He might think I'm accusin him of stealin . . . and anyway, the walk'll do me good. Then too, them nesters with the bed . . . they might bring me home 'f I ain't no other way . . . and I wanta see the bed . . .

So finally he crept quietly back down the hill and started into town with a canteen on his shoulder and his hat pulled down.

seven It was noon. Nothing moved. The sun had burned a hole in the sky. Not even any shadows moving. They were fast to the ground as if caught on bobwire. Not even buzzard shadows trickled up and down the hills. In cover coyotes panted, their pointed tongues rolled toward the center from each side. Pack rats scrambled deep among their burrows of stolen sticks and stones. Snakes were laid up under the black of rocks. Trees just hung. Pinned to the sky by thorns and prickly branches. Dust stood thick over everything. Even when nothing else moved the dust moved. The heat did not bother the dust.

Flat against the ground something was moving. If you count bugs as something, then something was moving. Deep in the holes and cuts on the track little bugs were running. Once it had been a buffalo trail, the track, when the big herds fifty miles abreast spread over it following the scent of greening grass. Now the buffalo marks were gone, save for bones to mark which way they'd gone. The broad-hoofed Texas steers which bawled this way no more had stomped out the buffalo marks. The track was as it had been in the beginning when it had been a sea track and plant-like animals had been fixed along it and bugs no man had ever seen to hold had squirmed along it.

Something else was moving now. An eagle. Ragged-headed and hot it hung by the sun. But now it dropped, for there was something dark and lumpy it saw and the dark and lumpy something was moving too. The eagle thought it was something else. Something he used to see moving up and down the plains. Following the wind. Going where the grass was. Something black and fierce and bellowing. The eagle remembered back before the broad-hoofed Texas steers to the small-hoofed buffalo. It dropped down lower and kept wondering if it were that other thing. Eagles have no words for things like buffalo. It skimmed the ground and rose abruptly. Its eyes were bad. But now it knew that thing was not the other thing. It was instead the two-legged thing that was always there and wandered around hunting and digging in the dirt. The eagle *kacked* and lifted on its wings that faltered in the heat and then it hung there by the sun, hoping . . .

Hutch stopped. He stood bowed, the brass head of the bed sticking up above his hat and making shadows of vines thru the dust of the track. He looked down at his shadow. It was a round blob with no sharp points to it. But around it was the broad lacy shadow of the head of the bed he lugged on his back. It had sharp points. Skinny stems. Leaves. Blossoms.

My God, but it's big.

He staggered to lean back. Slowly he let the brass head down to the ground where it leaned against him and he leaned against it to keep it from pushing him over.

It must weigh fifty pounds.

He wiped the sweat out of his eyes with his fingers.

If I'd knowed how big it was I'd have fetched the wagon. Course I didn't know I was gonna cabbage onto it . . . so I couldna.

There was a patch of shade ahead. Fastened hard to the ground. Not moving. Just there. He sighed and imagined how cool it must be. He reached behind him and hefted the bed up again and started for the shade, but soon the bed was sliding and his arms were wrenching from their sockets and finally he set it down gently in the dust and tried to pull it to the shade.

Its big balls of feet grooved the dust, caught in the ruts, and stopped. He turned toward it and pulled again with him walking backward. He pulled till he thought his heart was going to burst and his lungs were drying up and then he felt the shade dappling over him and he sighed and pulled it just one . . . two . . . no, three steps farther and then he stopped.

The skin of his back still burned with the memory of the hot brass. And that's what it's like to be branded, he thought. He reached back to feel his thin blue shirt, but it was still there. No viney places were burned into it. No holes of balls. No leaves or blossoms.

He leaned against the head of the bed and looked at it again. It was maybe as tall as him. It had two heart-shaped curves and from them all the vines and curls went out and around until it made him dizzy. He tapped his fingernail against one of the balls and it gave a hollow sound. Rather like a bell. He liked the high clear sound of it. Then he had to tap a leaf and hear its ting and feel its ragged edges and its stem. Then he tapped a blossom, well, not a blossom, but a bud, a brass bud of a flower that would never open and he wondered what it would look like should it open so that he stooped to look up underneath and see if there was anything inside of it and if it pinged as loudly on the petal end as on the stem end. He finally straightened up well satisfied.

92

It'll be mighty and bright in the house.

He shook his arms and hands to get the sweat to dry.

It'll be mighty and bright in the house . . . *if I can get it in.*

He worried about this some while getting out the calico rag and wiping his face and then tying back his hair with it.

What if the roof ain't high enough? But then he thought, *I* get in the house . . . so it's high enough. But what if the room ain't big enough? I guess I could make it bigger.

He thought about that awhile, about having the house with a wall pulled out and things running in and out free as you please and badger eyes and chins propped on the ripped up sod and watching him and something was likely to walk right off the hill behind the house onto his roof which would give way without the wall and the something on the roof would come kiting and screeching right down in his face with its big dusty foot. . . .

Might be better to build on another room. A separate room. Make a dogtrot in between. Yeah . . . that'd be better.

He slipped the clay bottle off his shoulder and took a drink, the water running down the dusty wrinkles of his chin and under his shirt, and he sloshed some onto his neck and stood there with his shirt open to drip dry.

But what kind of a room would you call it? Just a room for a bed? Like in a hotel? I reckon it could be a room like in a hotel. Maybe I could even   rent   it   out. If I had some beer and a dancing girl (which I ain't) and a cardman to play games (which I don't know how or where to find one that would come) and if the herds were still driftin up this trail (which they ain't) I reckon I could let it out. Only . . . don't know who'd want it.

He crossed his arms and studied the sky, afraid to even

put the next thought into words now that it was October, but late this month, or maybe early next month, he'd go down to the fort again to see if Dittany had come home. He'd lost count of how many years it had been since she was taken by the Sye-ox, but he'd never given up hope that someday she'd come home with her little doll of cornhusks and buckeyes and whang. It was partly why he'd stayed there all these years digging in the dirt he didn't think much of while wagon trains and fur men and gold seekers rushed on past and let him watch them wistful-eyed.

Never found her little bones . . . nor thread of dress . . . nor the pretty little doll with its yellow hair, furry skirt and beads and buckeye face with happy painted on . . . *she'll come home.*

A bird fluttered the limp leaves of the tree above his head and then dropped to his feet where some water had dripped into the dust and left a darkish place. The bird opened its beak and leaned down toward the darkish place to drink, but the water was long gone and it brought up only dust in its beak. Hutch stooped to pour more water at his feet and the bird flopped into it with wings that staggered, put its head down, closed its eyes.

"That ain't how you do it," Hutch told the bird.

But the bird fluffed its feathers out, fluffed again with a jerking motion, dropped its head down lower and was still.

He stared at it awhile. Nudged it with his toe, then touched it with his fingers.

Now why couldna God have told that bird they's water not more'n mile off? I spose it's been settin here all this time when it coulda flown down to my stream and had a good long drink. Now that ain't fair. But he thought this last in tiny hidden words for it wouldn't do to criticize the Lord. I reckon He musta had a reason.

94

He kept watching it, hoping it would rise and fly away. He lifted its head with his fingertips, but when he let go the head dropped down again. He fanned it slowly with his hat.

"Well," he said, "it's not ever bird that had someone with it in its last minutes. You're luckier than most at that."

He heaped some dirt over it, but not over its head. He thought that even dead it might want to look out and see. So he just covered the body and left the head sticking out and then he dragged up to his feet and pulled the head of the bed on his back and staggered out of the shade into the burning sun.

He'd found the head of the bed down at the new nester's cabin. The nester was moving. He was moving because he was hungry and there were too many hoppergrasses and locusts and things that ate up a man's harvest. There was too much sun in the summer. Too little water. Too much wind in the spring. Too much snow in the winter. He and his woman were tired of too much of what they didn't want and too little of everything else, so they were moving either back east or out to California. They hadn't decided which and that was why they wanted to get rid of the bed. It was too heavy to lug back and forth. Their wagon too old. Their oxen too thin.

And it only cost me three dollars.

He shrugged and eased it higher on his back.

Of course he didn't have the three dollars, but he thought he knew where he could get it. He thought he could take his new pair of boots back to the store where he'd bought them and get his seven dollars back.

Seven dollars . . . my God, I musta been outa my mind!

But they hadn't a mark on them. Not even a scratch or a crease. He didn't really need them. Where was he going to wear them? He could ride the mule to town and carry M.

95

Gruber's boots (which hurt his feet) and put them on when he got to town, and if he was careful and didn't step too hard they weren't so bad. For home, he could make himself a pair of Shawnee moccasins if he could find a dead animal to make them out of. And then when he had back his seven dollars, he would go and pay for the bed and that would give him four left over.

I should never have paid so much for them boots. He bit his lip. But they had been so pretty and had different colors on them and were fancy stitched and he had kept looking at them and then they had been taken out of the window of Marshall's Store and one night he woke up suddenly thinking of them with his heart breaking and he had dug up the can in the floor and counted out six dollars (all he had) and taken it and tied it carefully in the corner of his shirt and ridden into town at dawn to be waiting when Mr. Marshall came to unlock the door. And Mr. Marshall had been good enough to wait on the extra dollar that he hadn't had and let him take them boots with him right then. How he had walked along the streets of Three Trails so all could see how his new boots shone in the sun. And only when night came with no moon had he taken them off, climbed back on the mule and gone home with the new boots snuggled in his arms like a baby.

What if he won't take em back? he thought all at once. Since he had to wait for the extra dollar and all . . . since he seen me wearin em that day and one time to church . . . though only one time, cause the old ones can do for church . . . but he might get mad.

He stopped and set the bed down again.

"He might get mad," he said aloud, "and what'll I do if he does?"

He sat beside the bed and let it tip to lean against his

back and felt cool streaks across his skin where the laciness of the brass shielded it from the sun.

Why should he get mad . . . they ain't hurt. Still, he *might* get mad. Let's see . . . if I took beans to sell to Mr. Marshall and he bought em and then later he said to me, "Hutch, take back them beans . . . I just don't want em anymore," I'd get mad. He puzzled.

He took off his hat and fanned himself with it. Let's see . . . I could p'tend like them boots was only six dollars and maybe Mr. Marshall'd be so glad to think that he was makin an extry dollar that he'd take em back. Or, I could offer to take a little less for em since they've been wore . . . say . . . five dollars . . . but that only leaves me two . . . not that it matters . . . so I lose two dollars, so I figure the bed costs me five insteada three and that's only two less than seven for a pair of boots and that's cheap for a boughten bed. My land. He remembered how the other beds were, those back in the cabin at home, those poled to the wall in some of the places they lived and those others that were just corn-husk and hide pallets. They wasn't really beds, he thought. This here's a bed. Them wasn't.

We call em beds, but they's really pallents, and that quick he was back in the cabin in Kaintuck and hearing his ma talking to a newcome woman, showing her about the cabin which wasn't hard . . . you stood in the middle and you turned around and looked from the pegs where they hung their clothes to the kettle by the cat-and-clay to the pun-cheon table to the benches to the open door and you were all around it. *Where I come from, his ma was going on, we had lots better'n this, but out here we just hafta put up with what we ain't got. My man is a preacher?* she ended it like a question in the North Carolina way. *A preacher . . . man of God . . . kin read the Bible . . . marries folks . . . sees they gets the rousements . . . and he says we're gonna have better'n this someday. In fact, he has gone and writ a letter to get us a real bed like I had when I was a girl? Up again. You know we lived, my folks and me, in a love-ly home . . . it was brick? We had slaves, course. Though, my daddy didn't believe in slaves everyone did it and 'f you didn't you just couldn't make it with a big plantation like we had? Carr was our name and our place was called Carr's Castle? Course it wasn't really a castle but my mommy's mommy come from England and she lived in a castle . . . fact while I was a young'un yet tended to by a black mammy with a scarf round her head, a letter come from England and it says that our folks over there was all dead and had left us a castle which was our family home. Of course my mommy wanted the worst way to go and get it but then my daddy said, "What you want with that . . . look what we've got here."*

Hutch sat on a pallet alongside the baby. He poked his finger at her and he pretended he was only playing with the baby, but he was listening. He wanted to see if his ma would tell the story any different. Sometimes she made it even grander. It depended on the person she was telling it to. If it looked like they'd believe anything, then she added on to it. But if they looked like they might be able to read and write a little, she was more careful. It was a lie, no matter how she told it. Hutch knew the little shake house his grandparents lived in and their wornoutness from grubbing in the dirt.

"Eena, meena, mona, mite,
    Basca, lora——"

"Stop it, Jabal!" His ma turned away from the stranger woman, using his calling-name. "Stop teachin that baby silly talk."

"Grandaddy says it," he slipped back a little to be out of reach of her long strong arms.

"And quit callin that old tramp your grandaddy. He ain't no such a thing. Your grandaddy's long dead, rest his soul. That old tramp!"

She turned back to the woman, her hands reaching out for the kettle to set it closer to the fire and warm the tea that had been steeping all day.

"He ain't no old tramp," Hutch said softly, thinking maybe she wouldn't whop him with a stranger in the cabin. "He's a hunter and he's seen the ocean——"

"He's a liar, that's what he is. Dirty old drunken man. Filthy old man comin round to the cabin beggin somethin to eat all the time. If he's a hunter whyn't he go out an ketch somethin to eat?"

She stepped toward him, her hands hanging loose now and almost on a level with his head. Her back hid him from the stranger woman who sat now on a log bench by the fire. "Tell me that," she said, "whyn't he?" She was tall. Taller than common. Her face was lined. Her skin was dry and peely. Her hands were dry and peely too. They were also wrinkled. Her hands were like a man's hands. She wore a knot at the back of her neck. Her hair was no color at all. Just hair color. Her eyes were like the sky when it is raining. Her mouth was big.

"Get outside with your silly talk . . . get out and take the baby with you."

He picked up the baby and stepped carefully around her, staying out of her reach and never taking his eyes off her. He carried the baby a good way from the cabin before he set her down. He carried her till he heard marsh birds calling. Out there there was a swamp smell and it was very musky. Earthy. Wet. Like beavers and minks and otters and muskrats and wet flowers and moss and spongy earth. The trees sighed with the wind. When he looked back he could see the cabin light far off, just the window shaped light, hacked out with an oiled hide crammed in it. Then he was safe. Both he and the baby were safe where neither had to be afraid.

Everyone calls him grandaddy, he said stubbornly inside his head. He is so a hunter and he has so seen the ocean. He ain't neither a liar and *he* don't stutter. When I get big, I'm gonna be a hunter and see the ocean. I'm gonna have blue ropes runnin down my arms and a long beard like a Shawnee cape. And I'm gonna cuss when I want to. I'm gonna walk right up to them, to her and pa, and I'm gonna say *Goddam!*

"Shucks."

Now he pushed some pebbles with his toe and one pebble stuck in his old boot where the sole was parted from the upper and he could feel how hot the pebble was against his big toe and he reckoned the pebble was glad to have something cool against it. He let it stay awhile, then reached down and dug it out.

"Shucks," he said again. "If that ain't just like a young'un . . . wantin to be mean to their blessed ma and pa . . . and for nothin. Whatever comes over a young'un to make em so spiteful and spiteful?"

Reckon if I say six dollars . . . ? I paid six dollars for em Mr. Marshall three months back and they just don't fit. He flushed. That's a terrible lie, he told himself. The Lord'll know and what'll He think of me? But I can't say, Looky here, Mr. Marshall . . . I want a shiny brass bed more'n the boots and so I wonder could I fetch them boots back?

He sighed. It was so wrong. Everything a man thought was wrong. Now wantin . . . it went against the ninth . . . or was it the seventh . . . sixth commandment . . . *Thou shalt*

100

not covet. Yessir. Even a little innocent looking thought like wantin two things at the same time, like the bed *and* the boots, even that was wrong. It was a wonder when you thought about it that anyone ever got out of this world and into heaven with so much to remember while having to live life at the same time. He sighed. Reckon sixty years is bout as long as a man kin hold out.

I'll say, I paid seven dollars for em Mr. Marshall. And then maybe he'll take em back and give me seven and if he won't give me seven maybe he'll still take em back and give me somethin. Why couldn't he just lend me the three on the boots and then later when I had the three again I could go and pay him back?

He wondered which would be best, to give them up altogether or to trade them back for money? Which would look best? Which would make it look like he wasn't so poor?

They'll just have to go back.

He craned around and looked at the head of the bed. He wasn't halfway home. He could still pick it up and cart it back. He could still set it back in their dooryard and say, Guess I don't really need it. I was thinkin . . . ain't got room for it . . . and I'll just have to build me on an extry room and what with it gettin to be November pretty soon when it's so dry and all and the ground hard as a skillet so that I would hafta wait till next spring and that would mean the bed'd hafta set outside thru the winter and somethin might happen to it . . . prob'ly ruin it what with snow and ice and all . . . But what would they think? They'd think I'm old and addled and poor, that's what they'd think.

He staggered back to his feet. Took a deep breath. Straightened his shirt. Slammed his hat back on his head. Fanned himself with his hair a time or two.

Naw . . . she talked like they needed the money anyway. She didn't really say. But a man kin tell. A old man, he kin

101

tell. And she looked like she might be . . . and anyway, they're just young. Just startin out and havin their own pitiful troubles . . . reckon I kin get the money somewhere and I'll just keep the bed.

He squirmed his back against the head of the bed and lifted it and started on. Lizards were out now. Birds were moving around a little more. He saw two buzzards drifting. Shadows were fluttering a little too. A tiny wind was coming from somewhere. A small herd of dainty-hoofed antelope broke cover and crossed the hills to his right.

As he walked bent low he kept his eyes on the track. Partly to keep his mind off the weight of the bed and partly to keep an eye out for money. Maybe a gold piece dropped there sometime. Trail hands used to go up and down it. Maybe one of them had a gold piece and dropped it. (*Whereat did you lose it?—Dunno, long here somewhere. —Aw, come on . . . they's plenty more when we get these beef to Dodge . . . come on.*) He nodded to himself. Could be. He could see how it might have happened. Sure. Maybe even some settler on his way to buy sugar and flour. (*Joe, I tolt you and I tolt you not to just stick it in your pocket . . . it's all we had and what're the kids gonna eat?*) He clucked his tongue. Them poor young'uns. Maybe someone else had dropped it, maybe a long time back, maybe a feller with a Spanish shield of gold and a high cantled saddle and big rowels clankin and he would never miss it. Maybe it was hidden under the dust and the winter snows and the buffalo had tromped over it and then the Texas herds and even the settlers but no one had ever seen it because God was waiting for him to be born and walk along that track and find it. God was going to lead him to it. He was going to lead him to it and point and show him *There it is, you need the money and so I pervided for you, My son.*

He believed it was possible. He believed in God's wonders and that He saw and personally knew by name every little brown sparrow and he was certainly a sparrow. A sixty-year-old one maybe who wore clothes and talked like a man, but nevertheless, a sparrow. He believed that even if no one had ever dropped a piece of gold on the trail God could throw one down if he wanted to, and if he didn't, then there was a reason.

And by the time he came in sight of his cottonwoods and buffalo bushes, he knew there was a reason, for no gold had been turned up by his sharp pointed eyes. He was not really disappointed. It just meant he had to get the bed on his own.

He set the bed down by his door and went into the cool of the house. Water was standing in the bucket just inside the door and he drank from the dipper and then poured some over his head and shoulders and felt it trickling down his neck. He wanted to lie down and rest, but he wanted to get the other half of the bed now. Right now. He wanted it to look at. To touch. To set up here in this room. To lie on and think.

So he whistled down the mule, hitched it to his two-wheeled cart and turned it north. It wasn't hard going when you were riding. He marveled at how the land went by. How slow it was walking and how fast it was riding. How the whole world seemed to go by so fast with the jog of the mule. There was where he had stopped and thought about taking the bed back, and there was where he had thought about his ma saying "pallents" and there was where he had considered lying to Mr. Marshall and there was still the poor dead little bird in its mound of dirt. How fast he caught back up with it all.

He half hoped that when he got back they would be having supper and they would ask him to join them in a bite.

Just a cup of coffee and maybe a little soup would be fine, he could hear himself saying. And he surely would remember to take off his hat and wash at the basin. He didn't always wash at the basin when he ate at his own place, but out among people it was the nice thing to do.

His tongue was all set for soup by the time he got to their place. But no one asked him for anything at all, because no one was there. Their horse and wagon was gone and he reckoned they'd gone into town for supplies or maybe to see some other folks and tell them good-bye and he was sorry it wasn't him they were telling good-bye because he'd have offered them some coffee and some soup and even beans and they could all have sat around and talked late and maybe even stayed the night.

Stayed the night.

How long had it been since someone stayed the night? Why, never. He'd always had the hope that someone would come, especially in a winter storm, and stay the night. Maybe two, three, thirty nights. It would be so pleasant. So friendly. He thought how they would eat together and the night would wear on but there would be nothing to fear in the dark and they'd talk slower and slower and then they'd lie down on their pallets and the sound of their snores would mix. No, not the sound of their snores, the sound of their breathing, for he wouldn't snore. Probably wouldn't sleep the first few nights for fear of keeping his company awake with his restless turning and for fear they might want something in the night and he wouldn't be awake to jump up and get it for them and for fear they might wake and be afraid in a strange place and would want someone to talk to.

"Well," he sighed.

He finally loaded the foot of the bed and the side rails

and the mattress and springs and then he waited awhile longer, hoping they might still come home. Hoping to see their wagon jigging along in the dusk and her shawl flapping out and his hat bobbing with the wagon's pitch. But though he waited till night, they didn't come. It turned dark. Full dark and the coyotes cried in the hills and the moon was slow to come. At last he left, pushing to their door and dusting out his tracks in the dooryard just to be neat.

And in the night he started for home with the other half of the bed glistening around him in the soft moonlight.

But he hadn't gotten far when he thought he heard someone following him.

Could be them nesters, he thought hopefully. Maybe they come home . . . found the bed gone . . . said, "Shoot, we meant to have the old man stay for supper," and now they's catchin up to me. He whoad the mule and turned to wave. "That you, Wilkerson?" he yelled into the muddled shadows of the night where the moon lit the open plain so dimly that coyotes, rocks and buffalo bushes all were as one. "I'm here," he yelled again. But no one was rushing toward him thru the soft moonlight and no voice called back to him.

He twitched the reins and the mule started up again. But when they got to where the bird had died he was certain he heard something again. He waited till they were under the dark of the trees before he hauled the mule to a stop. This time he didn't yell but even took off his shirt and draped it over the brass that stuck up beyond the top of the cart so the shinyness would not give him away. He stared back over the trail till his eyes began to water. But there was nothing there.

"Wonder . . . reckon it could be that old hunter that's up there in the hills," he whispered. "Ain't heard no guns nor nothin . . . maybe he's hungry . . . sick . . . maybe he's seen me and the mule and . . . they say he's such a ornery cuss and he's wanted . . . still, if he's hungry . . . sick . . . maybe . . ." he wheezed and took a deep breath, "That you Mr. Rapaho?" he called. "That you out there?" But still there was no answer unless you count an owl hoot as an answer.

"Come on, Mule," he hunched down now and picked up the reins again. "Let's get on home." And he made the mule step it up so that the rattling of the cart and the rattling of the bed and the rattling of the hoofs drowned out the small timid steps which followed them.

eight

He fetched a lantern outside to light the dooryard and began to put the bed together. As he worked with it, it gave him a new feeling. He was kneeling, squatting, walking crouched all around it hooking the balls and sockets of the head and foot together and everytime he touched it it seemed to grow more magnificent. Bigger. Brassier. Grander. Till it seemed to be towering above him and reaching clear into the sky and even beyond the moon and wheeling stars.

Out on the ridges coyotes cried but he felt no kinship with them. Not this night. He was different this night. He was set apart by this thing a man's hands had made for kings to sleep on.

It was hard to work it all together for it was so big, so heavy, and one end of it would topple just as the other end was fixed. But he didn't care how hard it was to set it up. In fact it pleased him.

No coyote could put it together.

Several times he had to stop and turn the wick up in the lantern and each time as he stood away from the bed and just looked at it growing there in the night, he saw himself standing in the ranks of bootmakers, bankers, merchants and men who were respected—for they slept on beds. He saw himself as a general leading armies—for even in the field of battle generals carried beds with them, he'd heard. He saw himself akin to kings—for kings were always born and always died in beds. Even though he could barely read and write and was a poor dirt farmer and was often frightened of the dark and other things and men and had not even the money to pay for this bed, he was like the rich men and the generals and the kings for he was going to lie down in a bed for the first time in his life as they were lying on theirs even now.

And then it was together. It was a little weak. It shook some when he leaned against it. But it still reached beyond the moon and stars and he was awed by it, by the way it cut the moonlight into viney pieces and caused the wind to whistle and break apart. He had to hold onto it a moment for he was shaking. And he had to fight for his breath a little for it was so . . . there was no word. And he had to finally kneel beside it because he was humble that this night he was to enter the brotherhood of men who were not.

But when he gently eased it to the door, it wouldn't go through.

Why didn't I think of that?

And he was ashamed because a merchant or a general or a king, he would have thought of that.

But I ain't belonged among em long.

He began to take the bed apart and carry the pieces inside. But there was not room for it in there. Not with the harpsichord and the two velvet chairs and those with and without arms and the claw-footed table and the cracked mirror and M. Gruber's trunk.

They just ain't room.

He took the pieces of the bed outside again and he was so disappointed that he had to lean against the foot a min-

ute and cry a little. But then he straightened up and began
to set it up again. He would set it up out where the moon
and stars and cottonwoods and coyotes could see him sleeping on it and know he was a man.

I gotta sleep on it tonight. What if Mr. Marshall won't
give me the three dollars . . .

Again the bed towered above him and again he was in
awe of it and had to sit on the ground beside it for a long
time before he could bring himself to even think of getting
into it. It was a strange thing he was doing. An important
thing he was doing, this entering the thing which showed
he was a man and not an animal scratching a bed together
out of rags, hides, straw, grass, dirt and falling down to
sleep and growling in its dreams.

At last he climbed onto it carefully. It creaked in a mas-
sive way which impressed him and it fell down. He turned
the wick up in the lantern and put it back together again.
And it fell down again, this time the foot falling on his head
so hard it dazed him.

He stood back from it and studied it. It seemed to know
that he had no right to be on it. It made him ashamed. Before the moon and the stars and the coyotes and the cottonwoods, it made him ashamed.

I coulda asked how it was it went together . . . but that
woulda made me more ashamed.

This time he laid it out on the ground and inspected the
balls and holes they were supposed to fit, and he found that
one ball was missing and this was why it had fallen down.

His eyes began to feel crusty and his arms and back to
ache and at last he lay down beside the fallen bed and slept
with one hand on it. Sometime before dawn he crept back
to his own pallet in the house and slept again and dreamed
he was a coyote dug into a den.

109

In the morning he drank his coffee sitting beside the bed and staring at the place where the missing ball should be. He couldn't believe it was gone, but it was. He tried to think could he have knocked it off along the trail. But when he felt the broken place it was old, worn almost smooth.

It was old when we fetched it out here, she had said, her lips pursed tight and bitter. *Didn't see no reason 't all to fetch the dad-blamed thing, but it was his ma's.* She had said it like she didn't think much of a grown man lugging something hundreds of miles just because it was his ma's. *We ain't never even used it. We ain't got no room for it. And we sure ain't fetchin it back or out which ever way we're a going.*

He watched a prairie dog sitting up and whistling, running to sit up and whistle again. There was a little wind in the grass. A small cloud to the west, very far away and kind of torn.

They fetched it out here and she didn't want it and they never used it. The plain truth was they couldn't use it. It was too old. Its joints didn't joint. It was just a bustedy down old bed. A man who knew how to fix things might could use it, but that ain't me. And he thought of the shelf inside that was propped on boulders because he didn't know how to hang it from the wall.

That woman is a liar. That woman sold me a good for nothin bed for three dollars when she knows I'm a old man and three dollars is terrible hard to come by . . . she knows about my bobwire loss . . . she knows bout my corn year before . . . that woman is a damn and terrible sinnin liar and crueler than a serpent's tongue as the Bible tells us.

He felt hot not from the sun. The heat was even in his chest.

I orter take it back. Now I *know* I orter take it back. The Lord didn't throw down no gold pieces for me and He was trying to tell me even then . . . and I ain't got the three dollars anyway . . . and I kin keep the boots . . . and I kin say, *Looky here, this bed won't stand up by its ownself.*

He pulled back his foot to kick at it, but when he looked at it, It's so purty, even layin down with grass and ants. And then he saw one brass leaf of it was mashing down the gourd vine and he pulled it off the vine very gently and patted the vine.

Goddam.

He wanted the bed and he wanted the boots and he wanted the bed to stay there with him and stand up so he could be like all men.

Proud.

Maybe someone'll come along who kin fix it, he reasoned. Now who would that be? You know . . . bet I could prop it up like I done my shelf . . . sure, why not? I   could prop   it   up.

He laughed but his eyes were bitter and hurt.

They think they done fooled the old man don't they? They think they done cheated the old man. Likely they're settin at home laughin about it even now. *We sold that old man a bed that won't even stand up . . . that dumb old man . . . settin here all these years looking for his little sister that's been a captive of the Sye-ox since he was a boy . . . that dumb old man makin pets of wild coyotes . . . that dumb old man let the drovers cut his bobwire . . . that dumb old man ain't got no money . . . but he'll hafta get it cause he owes us. . . .*

He set down the mug of coffee, got up, wiped his hands on the seat of his pants, looked at the sun, went back inside and got his hat, came out and hefted up the foot of the bed.

They hafta go by the trail beyond the little hills . . . no matter which way they're a headin . . . though personal, I think they're headin to hell. . . .

111

He lugged the foot of the bed up the hill, then went back for the head. It would be handy if that mule was somewhere near, he thought and whistled hopefully, but it had skittered off the night before when he turned it loose. So he gave up hoping for it, and went back and got the side rails. It was noon then and he stopped and ate cold soup, and it felt good to have to eat cold soup for dinner, being in a hurry like a young'un.

By late day he had the mattress up the hill. Springs too. He found some boulders and he stood the bed up carefully then shoved it on the boulders. He chocked the feet all the way around and took some of his cut-up bobwire and wired it all together. He threw some grass against the bottom of the bed so it didn't show the boulders. Then he lay down on it gingerly. It held. He bounced. It held.

By God, wait till they leave. Wait till they drive by so smart with their bustedy Conestoga flappin its top. Wait till they drive by and see me layin here and I'll raise up and wave . . . *How de do* . . . and I'll be drinkin a cool cup of cold water. And I'll pull some branches and make a shade over my head and attach it to the bed. *Have a good trip and luck to you.* Yeah, that's what I'll yell when I wave. *The Lord go with you young folks if He can help steppin on the devil follerin you so close.* Yeah. *Have the bestus trip and write to me sometime.* Yeah, bet they can't neither one read nor write. *Be sure and write, cause I kin read and love to get letters from my* friends *and we got good mail service what with the railroad.* Yeah. That'll show em I ain't no old man they kin fool. By God, I'd have this bed set up for them to see if I had to nail it to the wind!

That night he washed and put on clean clothes and took a quilt out of M. Gruber's trunk because he wanted everything to be just right the first time he slept on a bed.

It was even grander than he thought. The stars rolled

over the bed and he watched them through the curlicues of brass and blossoms. The moon stood on the foot awhile. The wind whispered and whispered in his ears so soft. He thought of all the merchant men and bankers and skilled men who made wheels and horseshoes and could build things, and he saw them lying in their beds. He thought of the generals gone in their tents to sleep, and he saw them yawning on their beds. He thought of the kings taking off their crowns and handing them to servants who helped pull off their boots, and he saw them dreaming on their beds. And he felt that he belonged among them now.

Wish I'd told that drover bunch to go to hell, he thought. Who'd they think they were cuttin my bobwire. I ain't even sorry no more that that trail boss got himself drownded. Serves the bastard right! Cuttin folks bobwire. And he went on and thought about the Kiowas attacking the wagon train and he was sorry he hadn't gone out on the mule and fought because he thought he might have saved them all. There were lots of things he thought about but they were all explained in just five words.

I didn't have the bed.

He caressed it with one hand and felt a new strength in him. After a while he turned around and lay so he could see thru the head of it and he could tell how fast the stars were moving against the fixed points of brass. A coyote came near once, made curious by the curls and whirls of brass it hadn't seen, but jumped away when it scented him so close. And he nodded, for that's the way it should be— coyotes didn't belong on beds.

Yessir, he said to himself as he was slipping into sleep, it's worth the three dollars that I ain't got . . . and even then some.

He slept at last and dreamed that Mr. Marshall gave back the seven dollars and never said a cross word.

nine

Hutch stood outside Marshall's Store. He had on M. Gruber's best suit, the precious collar button and his own old boots. The new ones, the seven dollar ones, were wrapped in a clean calico shirt. He held them under one arm and pretended to be looking in the window at the assortment of pins and bullets and hammers and ribbon. Also in the window there was the headless form of a woman made out of black velvet. One shoulder of the form was uncovered while the rest of it was draped with blue and yellow gingham. Hutch couldn't look at it without feeling a little embarrassed. It wasn't right to have a lady's form in the window anyway, he thought, and then it with one shoulder sticking out naked to the world. He realized things were different from when he was a boy, but he wondered if the ladies who went inside to buy weren't a bit shocked when they saw the black velvet shoulder.

Mr. Marshall's business is sure gonna fall off.

He peered in through the window again, but there were still two men inside buying pants. He wished they'd hurry up and leave. He wanted to get it over with. He had practiced aloud what he was going to say and he thought it sounded pretty good. The mule had perked up its ears and jogged on faster. At least, it had seemed to think it right.

You see, Mr. Marshall, I been thinkin and thinkin and it seems to me I shouldn't have these boots cause I don't really need or go no where to wear em, cept to church, and I got boots for church. Good ones.

He looked down at his own boots and kicked some of the yellow dust off each toe and blew on the sticky patch he had painted where the scuffed places were.

You kin see for yourself, I don't actual need another pair. Likely, these'll last me and so I got to thinkin as how I don't need these new ones and they ain't hardly been wore at all . . . look for yourself . . . and ain't a mark on em cause I knew when I bought em I shouldna and I been careful with em and only wore em once to church and then I carried em over my saddle and put em on when I got to town . . . so you see I was wonderin how . . . that is . . . if I could trade for   something   else.

He stopped and studied over the words he'd heard in his head. Yes, that sounded pretty good. That didn't sound like he was poor. He hadn't asked for his money back, but only to trade the boots which he'd explained were worthless to him anyway. He was only going to ask to trade for something else. But it had to be something he was certain Mr. Marshall wouldn't have. Then he would say, Oh no! If you ain't got what I want there ain't nothin else I need and then they'd talk awhile and finally Mr. Marshall would offer back the seven dollars and he'd act like he didn't want it, but finally in the manner of one good fellow doing kindness for another and saving him embarrassment, he'd take it. And then they'd talk some longer. They might even go and have a beer.

Now that would be real nice. He seems like a tolerable nice feller and we might even have something to eat. Course . . . if he has to go home . . . other hand, he might ask me to dinner with him . . . at home . . . with him and his wife. Now that would be real nice.

Have more potatoes, Mr. Hutchinson, she would say, Mr. Marshall's wife. And they would be all heaped in a bowl with butter melting down thru the center which no one took because they were too polite and later she would eat the center in the kitchen while the men smoked.

No thank you . . . they are the best I've ever et, but I think not, ma'm. I would admire to, but look how my belt's already bustin—

No, that wouldn't do. He shook his head. A gentleman does not ask a lady to look at his belt. No, instead . . . I've had my plenty, thank you. Yes, that would be enough. Don't go on too much or she might think you're makin it up and not ask you back no more.

The two men inside had now decided about the pants and they were paying Mr. Marshall. He tucked the boots higher under his arm, tried to look casual and started in. But just then a lady brushed right past him and there she was getting waited on.

Hell.

He let his shoulders sag again and turned around and walked a few steps past the window. He spoke to the horses at the hitching rail, patting their hard heads and running his hand over their mossy noses. "Just like my chairs," he told them, "only green." He walked down the street a little farther, but it was hard to walk and keep seeing what was happening behind him at the store, so he turned around and came back up the street, but very slowly.

'F I only knew what it was I should ask to trade the boots for. And then he was sorry he had thought it up at all, because it was a dirty trick to play on a man like Mr. Marshall

116

who was going to take him home to dinner, but there was no other way.

See here, Mr. Marshall . . . I just went and bought these, and at the time I wanted em, but since that time I've found I need the money more——

Oh no. Land no! Hell no!

A rough dressed young man came up to Hutch. He stared at the bundle under Hutch's arm. One toe was sticking out.

"Whereat's the rest of him, grandpa?" the young man asked.

"Rest? Shucks," Hutch grinned slowly at the joke. "Ain't no *rest*. Pair of boots."

"Yeah?" The young man poked at the toe he could see. "I'm lookin to buy me a pair of boots. Wanta sell em?"

"Well . . ." Hutch tucked the bundle back a little farther against his chest. He saw the potatoes heaped so high in the china bowl and the house was so clean and had dotted curtains you see through. "I . . . uh . . . they ain't exactly mine."

"Ain't yours. What're you doin with em then?" he asked with interest. "Steal em?"

"No . . . shoot, no. They is mine, yet they ain't. That is, they don't rightly fit and I'm gonna trade em for some that does."

"Yeah? Let me see."

"Well," Hutch held tight his bundle, his right arm aching against the hard sole of one boot. "I don't know . . . that is, I bought em down there at Marshall's Store and I think he's got first right——"

"Come on, let me see em."

The young man pulled at the bundle and Hutch let go of it suddenly. One boot came out in the sun to show its fine stitching and wooden heel without a ding.

117

"Those are nice."

He stomped one on.

"Give you five dollars for em," he said, "in gold."

Hutch hesitated. The man held out the coins jerked from his jacket pocket. There it was, the three dollars and two more and likely Mr. Marshall wouldn't give him any more than that. He was already prepared to take a loss on them. But. He did want to sell them and here was a man wanting to buy and someone who didn't know him and would not speculate on it later and say, Wonder how the old feller's gettin along . . . maybe he needed that boot money . . . maybe I shouldn't give him no seed this spring without no money . . . but the potatoes shone like clouds on a hot day and there was a late vine blooming over the open window and it smelled like honeysuckle and Mr. Marshall reached out and offered him a cigar.

"No . . . No, I don't think so."

"Why not?"

"Well, I sorta promised. That is, if they didn't fit. I said I'd bring em back. There's another feller wanted em. The day I bought em he was standin there and he wanted em too, only I just happened to get waited on first and so I bought em but Mr. Marshall said to me, 'Hutch, if them boots don't fit you bring em back cause this here other feller wants em if you don't.'"

"Whyn't you try em on the day you bought em?"

"I was in a hurry."

"Oh. Well," the young man shrugged and handed the boot back. "Don't make no neverminds to me. Seen better anyway."

And off he went.

Seen better. Hutch mouthed the words after his swaggering figure. I doubt it. You're a bigger liar than me. *Seen*

118

better. Ain't never had your hands on any as good. *Seen better.* He spit.

He shook the boot the young man had had on his foot. He looked inside to see that it wasn't hurt. Wiped it off with his sleeve, then polished it with his hand.

He walked slowly back toward the store. Let's see. What wouldn't he have. Kerosene . . . whiskey . . . sugar . . . bullets . . . what? What's the hardest thing to get out here? What is it everybody wants but can't get? Windowglass. Yeah . . . windowglass.

You see, Mr. Marshall, I've got a hankerin to have me some windowglass so's in the winter I kin see out some. I hafta light a fire all the time in the winter (course I'd have to have one anyway for the heat). I hafta have a bigger fire than I need for heat in the winter time cause I ain't got no windows light kin come thru. I got to thinkin if I had some windowglass it would be so nice and I surely do need it more'n these boots which I've already told you about, though they're right nice boots, none better. But I do need the windowglass more. . . .

He nodded. That was it. That sounded good. That's how he'd do it. And then Mr. Marshall would be so sorry he didn't have it, and they'd talk awhile, and then the potatoes . . . dotted curtains . . . cigars. . . .

An hour later he came out of the store crestfallen and in his arms a piece of windowglass.

If that ain't the hell's luck. And he never even asked me to go with him and have no potatoes. How in hell could I know some windowglass just come in. The hell's luck!

He walked down to where the mule was tied holding the glass in front of him. The mule tossed its head just then and almost hit it and he jerked it back out of its way.

Hell's fire, if that ain't just the hell's luck.

I surely do understand, Hutch. Ain't nothin worse'n money throwed away on somethin you don't need, but you're in luck because this just come in and you're the first person to buy any. Things must be lookin up for you out there if you can buy a windowglass . . . and I'll just charge the diff'runce to you . . . you're good for it I know.

Hell's luck and goddam!

He clambered up on the mule and reached down and picked up the glass where he had leaned it against the hitching post. He looked thru it as he rode and he kept thinking, That son-of-a-bitch . . . what in hell would make him think that anyone out here would want a goddam fool thing like a windowglass?

They'll start callin me the rich Mr. Hutchinson. He snorted. And them crooked goddam nesters that sold me that bustedy bed'll go around sayin, "Did you know the rich Mr. Hutchinson owes us three dollars?" And then some wild-eyed crack-brained halfwit'll come along and murder me in the night for the money I got in my sock. And when he don't find it they'll all start sayin I found gold in some of my hills and men'll come a runnin from all over the world to dig up my hills and when they don't find it they'll start callin it The Mystery Mine and maybe even dig me outa my grave.

Hell's fire.

They went along. The mule clomping, mad because he wouldn't let it stop and graze. A buzzard followed them a ways. Two doves in a fight flew past. The sun turned cooler.

If I even knowed what to do with the damn stuff, he thought at last. How in hell do you get it in a hole in the wall? No, I couldn't ask. Hell no. No, I said, Where I come from everyone had windowglass. Ma was always proud of hers and kept it shined good with a hide and had cur-

120

tains of dotted stuff and mounds of mashed potatoes with butter dripping down the middle. But Mr. Marshall had only smiled polite and hadn't said, Come home with me . . . my wife's got mounds and mounds of mashed potatoes. . . .

Goddam dumb man, buying trash like windowglass for poor folks to lose their money on. Like throwin it away. Like sayin, Here wind . . . come get my hard earned gold.

"Watch where you're goin," he snapped at the mule. "You clumsy high-hoofed jackass."

He gripped the glass hard, sometimes changing hands, and it sometimes slipping.

Nine dollars it cost. And I still ain't got the money for the bed . . . not that they deserve it . . . damn thieves is what they are with their bustedy down old bed . . . and I don't have the boots. . . .

When he got home it was dark and an owl was calling. A wagon was pulled up in his yard and the nesters were siting in it.

"How do," he said polite as he could, climbing down from the mule with the glass.

"We need the money now," the woman burst out sharp-tongued.

"Hush . . . Hush," her husband said.

"Well, I ain't got it now," Hutch said.

"Ain't got it!" she said.

"That is," he propped the glass against the gourd vine. "I hafta go back in town to get it."

"Whereat you get that glass . . . it don't grow on trees . . . Arcy, d'you ever seen any glass trees?"

Her husband shoved her but she would not be stilled.

"I been to town," Hutch admitted. "I ordered this here glass and I got word it just come in, so I went to get it fore it got broke or somethin happened to it. I fetched it home

right off, fore I remembered bout your money . . . but I'm
going back tomorrow——"

"Whereat? Whereat you gonna get any money in town?"
She turned to her husband. "I don't b'lieve he's got any
money in town. Where would it be at? They ain't no bank."

"Mr. Marshall," Hutch stuttered, "he owes me . . . for
some beans . . . but he wasn't there . . . I'll go back tomorrow. . . ."

The woman threw her shawl around her and pressed
her mouth together. Her husband just stood first on one foot
then the other.

"By the way," Hutch said, "bet you didn't know that bed
don't set up too easy. Part of it was broke."

They looked at him blankly.

"Course I know you didn't know . . . I got it fixed . . . good
as new in fact . . . prob'ly better. . . ."

He waited. He thought they might offer to take less than
three dollars. But they said nothing.

"Well, I'll fetch it to you tomorrow."

Doubtfully they climbed back in their wagon. Hutch
watched them go. And after the sound of their horse's hoofs
died out he remembered that he hadn't asked them for a
bite to eat, and he had always thought how nice it would
be . . .

Other hand, he turned back to the house and lit a lamp.
Other hand, damn thieves . . . I hope they starve. *We need
the money now!* He remembered her voice's shrillness.
"What the hell for?" he asked her. "You settin sail for England?"

ten Hutch did not sleep on the bed that night. He was not fit. He did not belong among the merchants, rich men, generals and kings.

'F I did, I'd have got the three dollars.

He lay on a pallet of hides beside the bed where its moon shadow fell over him and he could touch the brass leaves.

All that piddlin around and lyin . . . terrible lyin . . . to that feller that wanted to buy them boots (and I shoulda let him have em) and to that damned old Marshall (ain't never gonna call him Mister again). Just like somethin an animal would do. Not like the way a man would do. No, no man would do like that. He'd go in the store and he'd say, *I don't want these damn boots and gimme back my money.* And after I said that I shoulda gone on and said, And while you're about it you shortchanged me when I come to buy sugar last time and I knowed it too but I just thought I'd wait and see how far you'd go and By God, you've gone too far!

Yeah. He's been shortchangin me for a long long time, and me always just a standin there like a fool and *lettin* him. Just smilin nice and sayin dumb things like, Ain't it a purty day. And out of the tail of my eye seein how he

123

counted it out so quick that I was always shorted some. I know why he done it. First, he done it cause he's a thief. And second, he done it cause I buy a lot on credit and he wants to make sure he gets ever last cent I owe and then a few. I'm payin more'n most folks just to live in this glory hole of a dirty dusty hot ugly flat empty-gutted country. And what for?

He pulled himself up with a brass blossom and stared hard at the towering bed.

"Tell me what for, you brass wonder! What for?"

The bed gleamed softly in the faint light. Its vines went in and out but never got to anywhere. Its leaves glittered their edges at him. Its blossoms opened to show their tongues of stamens.

He patted the bed gently.

"It ain't your fault, I guess," he said. "It ain't your fault I don't belong with kings."

He lay back down and looked up at the sky. But the sky could be a bore. He wished it would do something different or go away forever and something else sit there. At least there were some grey clouds in the sky and once in a while they blotted out some star or other. Once he saw an owl pass over lowly, its wings whispering like the grass. A few bats chittered out of cave somewhere and darted up and down after tiny bugs dancing like motes in the moonlight. A pack of coyotes ran to the west of him giving their sad sad cry.

'F I could at least belong with them. With somethin. Somewhere. Seems like I don't have no belongin no place.

The Big Dipper ticked around its constant circle and he watched it.

Just like me, he thought, goin around and around and never gettin no place at all. All its life . . . all my life . . . all

124

my life . . . damn life. What a cheap trick it was to let me play there in the dirt when I was a young'un and let me think I was like any other young'un, but to know all this was head of me. Yeah. You know Who knowed. You know Who.

All them dreams I had. Dreams and dreams . . . and dreams. . . .

Keelboat dreams and them boats ridin so loaded and low in the Ohio and slender as blacksnakes goin on down to the Mississippi. St. Louis where folks live in real houses and walk down real streets of stones and ever man's a king, a fur king comin and goin to the western mountains with the beaver in his boats and so rich he kin have hunderds pairs of boots. Wagoners' dreams and them wagons windin out toward Santa Fe with the remuda tended by a boy, and I coulda been that boy, and they say down there the mountains is peaky and purty and topped with snow and they's Spanish ladies and gentlemen and purty music whangin up and down ever street and lots of bright colors in everything but mostly they is red and ever man's a king there, too, what with minin silver and gold and turquoise down in Mexico and no one ever dares to cut their bobwire. San Francisco where they ain't so many ladies and gentlemen but they is lots of men and women and buildings painted gold and everything's on hills goin up and goin down so you gotta hold on tight and they's lots of Russian people wearing big fur hats and talkin words you never heard and ever man's a king with a diamond stick pin and the gold dust is so plentiful it drifts right thru the air and makes you cough and falls down in the gutters for them that want to bother brushing it up and dern near ever bed is made of brass. Mountain men dreams and places more beautiful than any other place you ever seen with tall pine woods and animals called elks and though they ain't no towns if you go far enough you kin see some of the northern sea where lives strange Injuns that carve a thing called whalebone and ever man's a king and no one steals water from another's stream. Dragoon dreams . . . Pony Express dreams . . . Trader dreams . . . and they ain't no end to wanderin . . . not ever.

Very pleasant hast thou been to me . . . them dreams . . .

But then he saw again the same old stars, a little dusty now with a wind kicking up, and behind them was the same old moon and there were no kings of any kind.

What a cheap and filthy trick, he thought again . . . let me play there in the dirt and dream them dreams and eat and chew them up and drink them down and never get no nearer to seein them before me. Standin there. There. Big. Real. True.

And I've been brought down to just one dream—a bed.

What a dirty and mean trick to make me think they was only mine and forever and that they'd come somehow . . . cause I believed they'd come . . . cause I prayed and was a good man and believed . . . cause I tried to right the wrong I done by waitin for my sister who likely is, he sighed, a fat and old old squaw all wrinkledy and greasy with lots of young'uns and grandchildren and all that and sets round sayin, Ugh. Yeah. That's prob'ly what she is . . . I've always knowed . . . but never said before that's prob'ly what she is and wouldn't know me nor remember me if I was standin right before her . . . Waited here for my little sister . . . here in this dusty hole with goddam bean and goddam corn that dries up and blows away . . . and goddam bobwire that someone cuts. . . .

Yeah. They'd come . . . the dreams . . . No, not this year,

I shrugged my shoulders each New Year's Eve alone and said, Not this year, but likely next. Damn dreams . . . damn cheap trick . . .

"Just a fool old man alone."

Day things began to wake like hawks and prairie dogs and antelope. The moon began to dull. The stars to fade. The east to light.

"But it's too late to cuss it now and change a thing."

He pulled himself up heavily and shoved his hat on his head.

Where did it go? I had it all. I had it all few days ago. But it got up and went and left me here.

"And all because of this brass bastard," he said to the bed. "You."

He stood unsteadily very tired with the pains that he so often had coming and going in his chest.

"I got to get the money somewhere now."

After he had some coffee and an egg and stale bread he came out of the house and felt a little better. It wasn't a hot day. The sun was nice, just warm. The sky was blue. There were some pinkish flowers blooming. The grass smelled like it had had a dew. The ground felt cool. The hills had soft shadows.

Wonder if he's still up there . . . that old hunter.

He leaned against the doorway's side and studied.

Likely he has money. All them hunters is rich. Yeah. Seen em lots of time plunkin down fifty dollars for a gun . . . buying sides of bacon . . . hats . . . boots, he winced . . . yeah, they're rich.

He watched a cloud of dust moving north and looking like mustangs.

Three dollars. He studied. If I could borry it . . . No. If

I could sell him somethin. Beans? They ain't worth a cup of coffee. Chickens? What'd he want with a chicken? Maybe in M. Gruber's trunk.

He went back in the house and lifted the heavy lid with its grapes and vines. There were lots of clothes. Shoes. Bonnets. Old papers. Books. A bracelet he had never seen before.

What about that old buffalo robe, he thought. Ain't much count. But he is a hide man. It was good once. Leastways I reckon it was good once.

He found it under the shelf thrown in a heap with ants walking up and down it and dust thick over it and a little mud caked on the bottom where it had been muddy when it rained in the spring.

Kind of poor like. Kind of old. Tatterdy. He brushed at it with his sleeve. Miserable lookin, ain't it? But he does go out for buffalo . . . think that's what he goes out for . . . that's what that poster said. Yeah. Said he was a hunter . . . said he drove a wagon covered with feathers and paint. Said he wore Injun sort of clothes . . . leather . . . fringe . . . beads . . . a eagle claw . . . said he was Wanted . . . Yeah. That's him.

He combed his hair and smoothed his blue shirt and put his yellow hat back on and started up the hill with the mothy hide slung over his arm. As he passed the bed he said, "Want you to know I'm doin this for you and that I'm scared to death of that old man."

Now what'd I have to go and think that for? I ain't scared. He's just a old man like me. Maybe somewhat ornerier. Maybe he has done bad things. But he's old like me. And if he kills me . . . what is there to lose? When you come right down to it . . . what is there to lose? Now.

128

But when he came in sight of the wagon with its red shafts and feathers blowing, he was afraid and hid behind the same boulder he'd hidden behind before. After a long time, he got up and went on toward the wagon timidly.

"Is anyone to home?" he called in a softer voice than usual.

But no one hallooed him back nor took a shot at him. There was no man. No horse or mule. Nothing but the wagon standing by itself in the sun.

He stood first on one foot then the other wishing he knew what to do. He walked around the wagon once and went to look beyond it. But there was only the silence of the sky and wind and no stir of dust that would mean a man or horse or mule.

Maybe I orter come back later when he's to home, he thought.

He left quickly when he made up his mind. He was sad that he had not settled anything about the money, yet glad that Rapaho had not been there because he was afraid of him.

All hide men and drovers and such like are such ornery cusses and always makin fun . . .

When it got dark he climbed the hills again and this time he took it slower because his back was hurting and his breath didn't come as it should.

But still no one was there.

He waited till he heard the coyotes run and then he started home. You might know he wouldn't show up when I finally went up there to talk to him. Just when I need so much to try to sell . . . they'll be comin, if not tonight, tomorrow for that money . . . what'll I say?

His eyes filled with tears.

129

It might as well be three hundred. Three hundred. Got as much chance of getting three hundred as I have of gettin three. Shoot. It might as well be three hundred.

The third hill down he had to stop and rest and he thought he heard the mule nearby and called to it, but it didn't come.

Derned independent mule.

He got back to the house and went inside, lighting his little oil lamp and setting it on the mantel.

Wonder what'll happen? he thought. Reckon they'll put me in jail? Or maybe they'll just take back the bed. But I don't want them to take back the bed. I want to keep it and . . .

He sighed.

Reckon I'll have to go to jail. Think you kin do that for a debt. And if I ain't gone long maybe Scoggins'd come up and look out for things . . . the mule (not that it deserves it) and the chickens (least they do give eggs) and the house. Maybe shut the door and see that no grass fire burns it down. Not that it could . . . don't think. And maybe I could give him somethin for it, but   it'd   hafta   be somethin   I   got. Not money.

He looked around at the precious velvet chairs, and the chairs with no arms, and the trunk of M. Gruber's, and the harpsichord, and the littler things such as the books, the newspaper he had bought but found too hard to read, the kettles and the candle molds, the poster pinned up by the fire to cover the ant tunnel.

Three Hundred Dollars.

He blinked and looked at it again and slowly spelled it out to make sure . . .

Three Hundred Dollars.

That's what it said.

WANTED
one buffalo hunter known
as
Rapaho
Reward
$300

He lifted the oil lamp down and held it close to the poster.

Age: 70-75. Height: 5'10". Weight 155. White hair. Grey eyes. Cheyenne dress. Wears eagle claw in ear. Painted wagon tied with feathers.

He squinted to read the smaller print below.

Wanted for murder New Mexico Territory.

Hutch clucked his tongue.

He don't sound like a very nice man. Still . . . they's always posters out on *someone.*

He put the lamp back and went to sit down in one of the velvet chairs after first taking the calico off the harpsichord and spreading it over the chair seat. He lit his pipe and leaned back and stared at the poster in the half dark.

Three hunderd dollars! But you hang for murder. Three hunderd dollars, and all I need is three. So, no, that wouldn't be right. But three hunderd dollars. I could pay the three . . . course they'd have to wait . . . and then I could buy some new bobwire . . . no, go up in the Black Hills and look for Dittany . . . no, just go. Just buy me a strong horse and get the hell to someplace else that I would rather be. And if the horse cost . . . oh, thirty maybe . . .

and some provisions to carry with me like maybe a new canteen and saddle blanket, and yeah, I'd need a new saddle. And some new boots. By damn, I'd go back to Marshall's . . . no. I'd go somewhere else where they's a man that's got some sense. Not Marshall. Hell with him. I'd get me a new hat, too. And a jacket. A purty one with fringe. And then . . . lessee . . . that'd cost about, oh, altogether bout a hunderd and I'd still have two hunderd left and I live on less'n that year after year so. . . .

But   I   do   think   they   hang you   for   murder.

Course . . . if he really did kill someone. It ain't right to kill someone . . . no, nor anything. But then maybe he had to kill someone. Maybe it was him or them. I've heard that sometimes happens amongst hide men and drovers and the like. And if it wasn't his fault at all . . . and he is an old man . . . older'n me . . . between seventy and seventy-five, that's what it said. And likely he gets tired same as I do. And likely things ain't so good for him now neither what with the buffalo all gone . . . and I've seen his wagon, oh, for years and years I've seen his wagon comin and a goin and he ain't never bothered me and look at what all I've got he'd prob'ly like to have. Why . . . these chairs and M. Gruber's trunk and the harpsichord . . .

No. It   would   not   be   right.

He heard the mule outside heading for the stable and the corn he'd thrown down.

Lessee . . . if I did it for Dittany. If I really went and got the money for Dittany . . . let them take back their damned old bed . . . with three hunderd I can buy lots of beds . . . and I'd take the money . . . I really would   and it   would   be   all   just   to help   find   her   my little sister. Yes. Just

132

for her. Just to set her free from the Sye-ox and the Black Hills and her dark little grandchildren . . . and she would wear a fine spotted and dotted dress with maybe a stripe round the bottom . . . and a bonnet, oh, yes, a bonnet with a flower and lots of feathers wavin from it like I've seen on fancy ladies . . . well, ladies anyway, and we would go away and live . . .

No. I   could   not   do   it. Not for the bed. Nor for Dittany. Nor for myself. Not never. No.

He slept inside this night because it was damp outside and he might have to give up the bed anyway and it was only harder to give it up when he spent more time looking at it.

He lay for a long time on his pallet by the fire and he thought quite a lot about Rapaho and he wondered if he had really killed someone and was he sorry and would someone finally turn him in and did his back hurt sometimes like his own did and had he any friends and was he ever so desperate for three dollars that he would even consider turning in a man for murder . . . a strange man that'd never harmed you . . . an old man . . . a tired old man who'd maybe had dreams too. . . .

No. I ain't gonna do it. Never. Mr. Rapaho, you are safe from me even if I go and lose the bed and hafta always live in this old dust hole.

eleven

He was waiting for them next morning. Time and again he walked out and stood to look down to the trail that he knew they'd take and he had it planned he'd say, Just take back your bed, cause I ain't got the money. And what if they did look at him cruel and even laugh. Maybe he deserved it. He had no right to the bed and he shouldn't have been so quick to say, "Sure, I'll buy it . . . three dollars . . . shoot, what's three dollars!"

Three dollars is an awful lot. Some men'd sell their souls for it.

It was another hot day, though it was late summer or rather early fall. But the sun seemed to have turned around and come back north to get a last spiteful bit of burning onto the grass that hadn't given up. The hot winds had cooled down. The shadows were longer and longer. Deeper too. There were lots and lots of clouds so that you could just stand in the sun and wait and a cloud would come along and cool you. You didn't even need a hat most days.

Finally he saw their dust and he went back in the sod house and got the little pack he'd made up in the morning. It had in it his pipe and tobacco and an extra shirt, a good one, one of M. Gruber's, and some leather to cut some Shawnee moccasins from, and some extra beans and all he had left of the bacon. He wasn't sure how well you ate in jail, so he was taking extra with him. And to help the time go by, he was going to make some moccasins for himself. Also because his boots were almost gone and he couldn't get thru the winter in just his boots.

He had washed up in the bucket and combed his hair. He had fed the chickens and the mule. He had hidden the collar button up the chimney in a leather bag. He wished he could hide the harpsichord, but there was no way, so he'd only pulled the piece of calico tight over it and hoped no one would carry it away while he was gone.

He went back outside and looked again and now the dust had a little dot before it, so they were getting closer.

He went back inside and wished they'd hurry up. He just stood. Everything was fixed the way he wanted to leave it so he didn't dare sit down on anything. He just stood, looking at the dirt floor where a beetle was dragging something after it, and no longer thinking of fancy things to say or lies or counting money he didn't have.

That's all over now, I reckon.

"Hey, Hutch." The voice called from his dooryard and he sighed, picked up the pack, stepped thru the door and pulled it softly to behind him.

"I'm ready," he said.

"Ready for what?"

It was Scoggins, the plowing neighbor that lived to the east.

"I . . . I was spectin someone else," he said.

"Well, I'm glad to see that you're all right."

"All right. Why wouldn't I be?"

"Didn't you know . . ." Scoggins' voice was excited. "Didn't you see it . . . the fire . . . last night?"

"Fire?"

135

"The grassfire. Was a big one. A real whomper. Come down out of the hills and blew clear in to Three Trails."

Hutch set down the pack.

"No. I didn't see it. I was tired. Sleepin."

"Shoot. You shoulda seen it."

"That why you come?"

"Yeah. And to say," Scoggins lowered his voice to a softer tone. "Course if you didn't see it . . . well, I reckoned you would want to know . . . that is, since they was friends of yours . . . and anyway, I need someone to help me dig the graves . . ."

"What graves?"

"Why, the Wilkersons. They got it . . . in the fire . . . went right thru their fields . . . house. . . . You could see where . . . that is, they went out in their corn patch hopin the corn was green enough not to burn, I reckon . . . they was out there in the field . . . but it wasn't green enough."

"You mean they're dead? The new nesters? The ones that was leavin? And she looked like she was . . . they're dead . . . they can't be dead . . . I owe em three dollars!"

"Well, you don't hafta pay it now."

Hutch stepped back against the house not noticing his feet were in the gourd vine.

"But that just can't be," he said. "I seen em just day before . . . they was here . . . and I said . . . and I . . ."

Scoggins took off his hat and fanned himself. He was sweating pretty hard. His shirt was dark in patches.

"Wanta help me bury em?" he said.

"I reckon."

Hutch picked up his pack and turned back to the door.

"Wait'll I drop this inside," he said.

He stepped back into the house where it was dark and cool. He went to look out the window where Scoggins couldn't see him. He was shaking and had to hang on hard

136

to the shutter frame. There was a terrible pain in his chest that came and went and felt like streaks of lightning.

They can't be dead. I owe em three dollars.

He went to the bucket and poured some water over his head and drank some too.

My God . . . I cussed them terrible in my mind . . . called em thieves and such like . . . wished em all bad luck . . . wanted to see em get hurt . . . yes, deep down that is what I wanted . . . But dear Lord God You wouldn't do a thing like that because I wanted it. No, You couldn't. Could You? No. Oh, no. Not for me. No. I ain't worth . . . no. I don't believe that had nothin at all to do with it. No. What I said . . . You know I was only mad . . . just a fool old man that was mad . . . counta them boots which I loved so much . . . and then the bed . . . and afraid I was gonna hafta give it up . . . Shoot, no. No. No.

"You comin?" Scoggins yelled out. "I'm burnin up out here."

"I'm comin."

Hutch climbed into the wagon beside him with his eyes down and his hat pulled low.

"What a terrible shame," he said. "What a terrible shame."

"Well . . . yeah . . . but I never liked em much," Scoggins said and whipped up the horse.

It took them into the night to dig the graves, for both of them were old, Scoggins just a little younger than Hutch, and both of them had to often stop and rest and stare at the day as it changed into night and the sky and it grew dark and then light lanterns to finish by.

The bodies were in pine boxes the undertaker had brought out from Three Trails. And when they went to put the first box down into the ground Scoggins set down his end suddenly.

"Let's look at em," he said.

"Look at em?"

"Yeah." Scoggins leaned close as if there were someone else who might hear. But there was no one. "They said you'd never know em for human. They said their skin was all turned black and the fat all melted from it and——"

"God's sakes Scoggins!"

"That's what they said."

"Who said?"

"Mr. Marshall and his wife. They was gonna buy some of their stuff and they come out here and they found em just all burned and twistedy too I guess and——"

"I don't wanta look."

"Won't hurt. Come on," he pried at the lid. "I'd like to see em. Just one, maybe, huh? Come on. They said looked like a Injun massacre——"

Hutch rolled his eyes sharp at Scoggins.

"You ever see a Injun massacre?"

"No."

"I did," he said. "My folks and all the wagon train was killed in a massacre. Don't wanta see nothin no more that's like a Injun massacre."

Scoggins hesitated.

"You don't hafta look," he said at last.

He pried at the lid again.

"Only take a minute . . . you kin turn your back. I wanta see . . . just once . . ."

The lid came loose and Hutch walked away and looked out at nothing. But back . . . far back and away . . . and over the hills to his right where the moon was rising . . . he was seeing an Injun massacre. Bodies turned black and twistedy . . . yeah . . . that's how it was.

"Hey, Hutch," Scoggins tugged at his sleeve. "Come on and look. I can't tell 'f it's the woman or the man."

Hutch turned, his eyes angry.

"Well, hell, I'd like to know. Wouldn't you like to know? Come on and look. It's somethin to see . . . it's all——"

"You make me sick," Hutch said and pulled away.

He walked down to the field where they had stood and the corn had burned and they hadn't made it because the corn was not green enough. You could see their footprints in the ground. Hutch lifted his lantern and looked to make sure. Yes, there were their footprints. Those they left behind. And there was the little locket that she always wore, its link snapped from the chain. And there was a handle like a broom handle and he reckoned they had tried to beat it out as it swept down upon them fast . . . so fast . . . he'd seen the grassfires and how fast they ran so that sometimes even a horse couldn't outrun them. He sighed and kicked at the footprints and threw down the handle of the broom that had not saved them. And there was   an   eagle claw   painted   red. He stooped and picked it up. It was like the one . . . the poster . . . the bounty hunter . . . naw, some Injun dropped this likely . . . but he put it in his pocket and walked back to Scoggins slower than he had left. He kept feeling it in his pocket. But Naw. Couldn't be. Why, he didn't even know them. Why would he? Naw. No. Still . . . it was a mighty funny thing.

Maybe he was hungry and he come down to try and buy some food and she smarted at him like she done to lots of folks . . . maybe she said, *Ain't got no food for dirty old hunters like you . . . 'f you can hunt whyn't you do it . . . whyn't you kill somethin to eat?*

She did remind me of my ma, he thought suddenly. I hadn't really thought . . . yet, I knowed there was someone she reminded me of . . . yeah . . . that sounds like somethin she would say. . . .

Still . . . that ain't no reason . . . no, no reason.

Maybe he come down and tried to steal their horse. That could be I suppose. Maybe somethin happened to his. Maybe it got a broke leg. Fell off a cliff. He had to shoot it. That could be.

But . . . that ain't no reason. . . .

Shoot . . . it's just a coincidence . . . it don't mean nothin . . . no, it really don't.

Scoggins put the lid back down now and pounded it with the hammer.

"Well, you're gonna be sorry you never looked. It sure was awful."

"How come ain't no one else here to bury em?" Hutch said.

"Ain't no one else, I guess. Dunno. Didn't have no friends I guess. Think you knowed em best. Think maybe you was their only friend."

Hutch felt tears coming in his eyes. To think they'd been his friends and he hadn't known. To think he'd been their only friends. And after all those things he thought . . . how he'd lie on the bed and wave as they went by . . . how he had cussed . . . thieves, that's what he called them. Thieves.

"Shucks," he said. "That makes me feel so terrible bad."

It was dawn by the time they got them buried and the ground mounded good. They made one small cross from the handle of the broom or whatever it had been and laid a rock on the other grave.

"Dear Lord," Hutch bowed his head, "we do commit these children of Your'n to Thy loving earth and hope that You will look out for them forever."

"That's enough," Scoggins said. "I never liked em anyway."

They rode slowly back to Hutch's place in the early morning sun.

140

"Have a bite to eat?" Hutch asked.

"Could use it."

And as Hutch built up the fire and set a kettle on he thought of how he'd always hoped to have someone come to eat and maybe stay awhile. But now it wasn't as much fun as he had thought.

I guess dreams is always better.

And as they ate he kept feeling the eagle claw in his pocket and looking at the poster by the fire and thinking how he was out of dreams and hopes and everything but maybe if he had three hundred dollars . . .

When I go down to the fort to see bout Dittany . . . dunno . . . maybe . . . go when the first snow comes . . and then maybe . . . by that time . . . cause if he really did . . . he orter hang . . . I think.

And later when Scoggins left and kicked the window-glass by the door, kicked it by accident, Hutch just sighed and gathered up the little glittery pieces and buried them under the gourd vine.

'Nother thing wouldna happened . . . 'f that old hunter hadna burned em out . . . 'f they weren't dead and needed burying Scoggins and his big splayed feet wouldna been here and busted my only piece I ever had of windowglass. Hell's luck. Man gettin other men killed and bustin their windowglass what ain't paid for. Hell's luck. And I think I orter turn him in . . . now.

✳ The settlement had crept closer to them till it was all around them now. People walked up and down. Just like they were walking on cobbled streets. Like they were home where there were horses. Like they were where ladies carried things over their heads to shade their skin and men wore stiff collars.

Some sat on their cabin doorlogs or on stoops of shaved wood. Though it was dark, there was nothing to fear. Everyone was here. Maybe during the day, some had been gone. But they were all home now.

Edsell's Store closed up when everyone went to bed, so a lot of people came and went to Edsell's Store at night. They didn't always have hides to trade or money to spend, but it cost nothing to look. Jabal's little sister liked to go over to the store. She would pick up some pretty from the counter and carry it around with her while she looked. When she left she always put the pretty back. It wasn't really very hard to put it back—she had had it for a little time just for her own. There was a lot of visiting back and forth, also a lot of map talk about good hunting places. Also a lot of gossip about roads being cut and schools being built. And when Edsell's Store and the map talk and the gossip wore thin, some would go down to Buskirk's, three cabins down from Jesse S., and stand there and listen while his wife gave him lessons on how to read. She taught him by the light of a lightwood stuck in the ground. Few of them could read, and none of them were ashamed of it when they were among themselves. It was when the traders came swinging thru, talking big, flashing little black books and writing down things on paper . . . (You say thirty hides . . . thirty . . . write that down . . . that's my bound boy . . . can write as good as any growed man . . . .) Then they were ashamed and looked at the boy bound and he was so small and not even married and he could write. They would count real loud when the trader talked about hides so he would know they could count. They would call out old Edsell to prove to the trader how good they could count . . . . (Ain't never yet had a man say he had forty hides in his pack and only give me thirty-nine or forty-one . . . .) But they never said anything to the trader about reading and writing. Only sometimes one would look over the bound boy's shoulder as if to question some thing he wrote, then nod to himself that it was all right after all.

It was very quiet as it grew later and Buskirk would put up the book and his wife would push the torch down in the dirt. The trees rocked and rocked from the high mountain wind. Women began to sing lullabys to babies. All up and down the clearing, when it was that time, you could hear the women singing. Sometimes they all sang together and made one big lullaby. Even the men liked to sing and would enter in. They all hungered for music when Jesse S. was out hunting. Jesse S. could make music because he had a fiddle, but no one else knew how to make it work or would dare to touch it. It was when Jesse S. was gone that they sang the most.

Peaceful slumbering on the ocean
Seamen fear no danger nigh . . .

The woman who taught them that song was from
the coast and her folks before her from England.
She said that everyone sang it on the coast because
so many men went to sea. She liked to tell how she
would go down with her mother every day to look for
her father's ship though it might be many a month
before his ship would come and they both knew it.
Still they would go down and look beyond the rocks
at the ocean. Stare. Hope. Watch and wait just as
anxious as if he might come in on that very tide.

Sleep, baby, sleep. .
Thy father tends the sheep . . .

But Jabal never thought too much of that one. He
liked the one best that was about the fox. His own
ma, when she was younger, she used to sing it. Before
she got all wrinkled and her hair fell back to hair
color and her hands got like a man's, she used to sing
it.

The fox went out on a wintery night
And he prayed for the moon to give him light . . .

But before long Jesse S. would hail them. He
would come stepping out of the deep woods with the
last peewee's call. He'd have fresh game on his back,
but never much, for he was no hunter. Jesse S.' wife
always defended him and took the meat real quick
and hung it in the back of the cabin where it
was dark so no one would see how many shots it took
to kill just one little deer or wild hog.

All were glad to see him. Especially if it were a

hot night down under the trees, they were glad. No one could sleep on nights that were hot, and the word would spread from the first who saw him all down the line and men would yell to their women tucking the babies in the sugar trough cradles, "Hey, Jesse S. is home." They would push their doors to against any wildcat or panther that might be skulking after their babes and they would go down to his cabin and sit around on the logs he had there and wait for him to hang up his rifle and pouch of shot and take off his shirt and then he would get out the fiddle and play for them.

The only trouble was, that sometimes he'd rather preach than play. He'd bow out part of a lively tune, then break it off and preach awhile. Then they would shuffle their feet and be downcast because they hankered for the playing now. Preaching was for later. For Sundays and for early eves, not for now. But the men would light another pipe and settle back and the women would wait with patient hands tucked in their skirts. But they didn't make their young'uns sit and listen. No, they wanted Jesse S. to know that preaching was for Sundays, so the young'uns ran after green fireflies and Shawnee ghosts and will-o-the-wisp and red foxfire and other things that young'uns run after.

Even had they dared to speak up to Jesse S. and say they didn't want any preaching, they wouldn't have dared to speak up to God like that, and Jesse S. made it clear to them that what they said to him went directly on to God. It would have been a terrible sin for which there could be no forgiveness not to want to hear about sin and God and the devil and heaven and hell especially when you were total alone in the vasty woods and expecting to die any day. You might admit such a thing in your secret mind. But never aloud. Why, it might make your cabin catch fire or your young'uns sicken or your man go huntin and not come back or the traders with their black books steal you blind. Because God heard all and he didn't forget. Jesse S. told them so. That was how they knew. He made it clear right from the start.

Well, it was second best to hearing the fiddle because of Jesse S. being gifted to rhyme. (Have you ever knowed a man who could rhyme . . . No, not me, nor a woman either, though once there was a crazy woman who—How dare you to say such a word. We're talkin about gifts from God put in Jesse S'. mouth.)

What Jesse S. liked most to talk about was Moses leading the children to the Promised Land. The men all liked it best. Some of the women liked it, too, though the older women that had been led to many and many a promised land by their hunting men, they set their mouths and didn't like it.

"Don't tell us about that, Jesse S." They'd smile, hoping they had what would be called a winning smile. "Tell us about people stayin put. Not everyone in the Bible run round all the time a huntin and a warrin and a seekin land that wasn't even theirs."

And because Jesse S. knew the women had power over their men he would tell them some quick story, sometimes the one about Sisera who was tomahawked by a Shawnee woman while he slept in her cabin. The women liked that story because they felt he had no business being in her cabin. But Jesse S. would always double back and sneak in Moses.

"And then they was told to make bricks
  'thout straw,
And when Moses heard it, it stuck in his
  maw

146

And he went to the Lord and he said,
  'Looky here,
Ain't no good to talk in Pharaoh's ear,
He looks at you like he cain't even hear.
You promised you'd set these poor folks
  free,
But talkin to you is like talkin to a tree
And you're only makin a liar out of me.
Now are we a goin, or are we gonna stay?
If things don't get better, they ain't gonna
  pray,
And he's got em makin bricks out of just
  plain clay.'
But the Lord raised His hand and he said,
  'Let me speak!'
And Moses cast his eyes down kinda meek.
And the Lord said, 'Who you think you're
  talkin to?
I've had bout all I'm gonna take from you.
I know what I promised . . . my memory's
  good.
I'm runnin this goin . . . Is that under-
  stood!' "

But when they saw Jesse S.' foot tapping, they'd yell, "Play us *Billy Boy*." And another would call out from the log shadows, "Play the one about the diamint ring." And, "Play the one bout green rushes." And another would yell, "No, not green rushes . . . green sleeves. "

So they'd sit in safety thru the hot damp nights with the trees rocking above them and the fireflies dancing round their heads and sometimes you'd see one disappear because a hand had caught it and was turning it over to look at it, and then you'd see it fly up again because the hand had let it go.

The women and the young'uns would finally go off to bed and long after Jabal's ma was asleep on her pallet, he'd wake and hear his pa outside, squatted down with a few of the men and talking about the price of pelts and the poorness of the game and the best way to run bullets and hounds and they were now living in a State and Tarnal!

Jabal would eye the dark that caught up under the roof and wonder if they were really going some more again and it didn't seem right because his middle brother was dead under the trumpet vine and it was tall now, and his biggest sister had got lost in the woods and never come home nor heard the horn they blew for her and the hounds couldn't track her beyond the river and he was almost thirteen and he didn't want to go anymore except back and away from his pa. Yes, he wanted to go back and away from his pa with his little sister and they would go over the Allegheny Fall to where they'd come from and no one would ever hurt them again.

✱ It came a dry spell in Kaintuck that spring. There'd been so little snow, there was no flood. Instead the crick banks stuck up dusty with a little reddish piddle in between.

"The dark and bloody ground give up its blood."

You know who said that—it was the preacher.

And after that the frogs came up out of the mud, which is where they always came from only we never saw them do it before. The fish turned up their bellies and washed against the dry-mouthed banks. Flies and every other thing came down to feed on them. Some folks got sores and a couple of cows up and died. Also a good old mud-and-plunger horse. Then the preacher said there'd come a storm (because that's the way it happened when it was Bible times and Moses and the Pharaoh and all that). And it did come up a storm, it came a heller with wind rain and hail and it topped a lot of trees that didn't need it.

Everyone was ready to listen then. Well, they wanted to go. But hadn't planned to yet. Maybe next year, you know . . . But they went quick when the preacher told them that the plagues of Egypt were upon them and they would have to get running or they'd never get to see the Sye-ox or the Promised Land.

He put it ever so good, dragging in the Lord and Moses and all that:

> "The Lord had filled them rivers with
>   blood,
> He'd jerked the frogs up out'n the mud,
> He'd blowed down dust, lice and flies
> Till them in Egypt couldn't see the skies.
> But still old Pharaoh sat on his throne,
> Though his land was gettin picked clean
>   as a bone.
> Now Moses was walkin round feelin blue
> When the Lord looked down and He said,
>   'Hey you!
> Get back in there and tell Pharaoh I said
> When I raise my hand, the game'll fall
>   dead,
> The squirrels, the fox, the deer and moose,
> Cause he ain't turned my people loose.
> And go on and say, Furthermore,
> The Lord wants them to explore
> To do his tradin, trappin, huntin
> Out where the land is there for the
>   wantin' . . ."

So they went. Like you were told before. Packed their plunder. Clicked up their horses. Never said good-bye. Just left on their tiny wagons that looked so big on the narrow traces thru the trees. Some went on horses. Some on foot. The older ones mostly went on foot, their wagons rotted, their horses dead from age, and anyway tripping across the Wide Mizzourye couldn't be any harder than the Allegheny Fall.

150

"Why, them Sye-ox ain't much farther'n Vincennes," the preacher promised. And though none had seen Vincennes they'd heard, and why, it wasn't far at all and was an outpost town, a frontier settlement with Injuns and just beyond, why, just beyond was the Mississippi and the Sye-ox Land.

So they headed for Vincennes sucking on the Wide Mizzourye with every tongue sweet as a bear tree's honey.

But Vincennes had buildings of brick and wood. It had cobbled streets. It had a cathedral. It had carriages with pillows. It had people who dressed like some of them remembered from back east. It was no frontier town, they said bitter-faced, it was growed a whopper. It was like a city. It had no Injuns campin in it. No scouts. No huntin men.

And they went on thru Vincennes with their eyes squinted straight ahead and the iron tires of their wagons striking sparks and hats pulled down and shawls pulled up so they could not see nor be seen by the fancy folk.

They inquired very soft of Jesse S. just how far off were the Sye-ox? But he only pointed west with his black hat waving its black ribbon west as well. No, he never answered them. He just went on before them in his ark with his young'uns flopping in the back of it and his woman lonesome-eyed and the rocker chair rocking by itself with its moon shining bright.

"St. Louis is a frontier town," he told them. "It's all frontier. When you get there they ain't nothin to be seen but frontier. Spread out far and wide far as the eye can reach is frontier."

And they saw it as the old frontier with lots of hills and forests and quiet birds and quick-footed game and nothing mapped beyond.

But St. Louis went and disappointed them being another town of brick and stone and wooden houses and glass windows. Well, there were some bearded men who were mountain men and who trapped in western mountains no man had ever heard of (so they were probably just lying) and who ran on rivers no man had known were there (another lie). "But you're lookin for the Sye-ox?" said the mountain men. "Lordy to God, the Sye-ox," they waved west, "they is way the hell and gone out there. That way. Yeah, out that way. Beyond." But the people were uncertain and they asked, "Beyond what?" "Why, just beyond, you tarnal fools. Beyond out there where they is, that's where beyond. To the beyond where they belong, that's where beyond."

So they rattled thru St. Louis with their eyes squinted straight ahead, after inquiring again real soft of Jesse S. if he knew just where it was that the mountain men had waved to. That is, exact. So you kin tell the pinpoint place, like point to it on a map.

"Map!" he said. "What map? Did Moses have a map?" And he waved them toward the west and his hat backed him up with its ribbon.

"Well," he said at last. "Reckon out round Leavenworth is where they is. And what is Leavenworth? Why, it's a fort . . . where you been you never heard of Leavenworth?"

But at Leavenworth they found they could not go any farther without a map or someone to lead them. That's what the man who headed the fort said. So they scrounged around and found a man who was just back from the great beyond and who didn't want to go back there again, but who said he'd go out with them for half of what they had and they'd have to buy some oxen too. So half of what they had they had to sell to pay him with.

It was pretty in the beyond where they had gotten to. It was frontier, though not with lots of sharp up and down hills and lots of forests or even birds and game like they had known. But it was pretty with rolling hills that rolled and rolled away just like the Wide Mizzourye promised in its song. And they rollereed away and across the wide Mizzourye where there were flowers all around and its was not too hot out in the sun. But it was stormy some, with storms that rolled the rolling hills and dropped water a foot deep all around them and tore against the flimsy wagons and scattered their miserable herd of scraggy horses and moaning oxen and the three cows out in the direction where the Sye-ox lived to hell and gone.

"Ain't this the Promised Land that we was promised and didn't get!"

Jesse S. again, dancing on before them with his hat waving its ribbon west.

But moving up the shallow Platte the Promised Land gave out.

There was less grass. There was more sand. Sagebrush and what can anyone do with sagebrush anyway? Alkalai dust rusting thru their lungs. No wood, save little dribs and drabs on sandy islands so that they had to learn to cook with buffalo dung and the women rubbed their hands over their hips and sighed at the things a woman had to do before she was dead at last.

They began to tire. It was harder than coming over the Allegheny Fall. It really was to hell and gone.

How far is it now, to where the Sye-ox is? they'd ask the preacher, and they didn't ask so soft. Why, just beyond them flats, I reckon. But every way they looked were flats and then they said, *Beyond what flats?* And, By God, beyond! he snapped at them.

And it would do you to remember it took Moses forty years!

And they began to wonder about the preacher . . .

They hit a dry spell like the one they'd left behind down in Kaintuck—sweet Kaintuck with its dark and bloody ground so soft and good to walk upon even though it's Stated. They would not have hit a dry spell except that Jesse S. insisted on swinging away from the river and looking for a short cut, which was none of his affair and he'd never been out there before and knew no more than they. But they didn't think about it when they agreed and followed him.

The scout looked at Jesse S. and his mouth was all sour and dusty and he said, "I told you so, old man. I told you this time of year you had to foller the river. But you wouldn't listen. Now here we are with lots of sagebrush and sand and no water that is fit to drink like we would've had if you had left things alone, old man."

The scout did not fall down with a thunderbolt in his throat from calling Jesse S. only old man . . . and they wondered . . .

They drank from buffalo wallows on their way back to the river. The wallows were muddy when they were at all. Sometimes the water would be all used up, slow to seep back if it came up from a spring. Never to seep back while they stood and looked at it if it came from rain.

Pawnees rode by and waved friendly. They waved back.

Is that the Sye-ox, they asked with some hope, brushing the hair out of their eyes and the dust off their necks. Is that them? But the scout said it was not and they went on. The Pawnees are so friendly, they said to Jesse S. Why can't we stay right here where we have already met the Pawnees and sit with them and smoke their pipe and hunt their lands? Why do we hafta go on to the Sye-ox?

But Jesse S. went on ahead of them without answering.

But then one of the friendly Pawnees got shot and killed one night sneaking around their horses. He was fixin to steal, they set their mouths at the scout. Back home we always killed the Shawnees when they was fixin to steal and in no time at all they learned not to steal. . . .

But the scout never even spoke to them. Just moved them out that night so fast and they left behind half of the half they had.

After they shot the Pawnee everything got worse. Horses ran off or broke their legs. Three young'uns fell off the wagon seat asleep and got run over. A woman died in childbirth. A man shot himself by accident. There was a fight and another man got shot and killed. A couple of women just up and died for no good reason. And they never had time to really stop and rest the way the scout kept running them. And to hell with hearing about Moses walking forty years. They reckoned they had walked two hunderd.

Other Pawnees must have found the dead Pawnee, for now they were Injun pestered. They were not shot or jumped but just followed. Them Injuns is so friendly, they told each other and waved. But the Pawnees had quit waving. Now they drove the game ahead of the wagon train so that they were hungry. They haunted the river banks and water holes so that they were thirstier. They howled some at nights so that they didn't get much rest. Beat on drums. Lit lots of fires. Set a grassfire just beyond their camp one night with the wind right to carry it over them. Ran a stampede of buffalo down on them.

We don't care how far the damned Sye-ox is, they

told Jesse S. then. We have got to the beyond where we are goin. We ain't goin any beyonder than what we have gone. Maybe we should go back to where we have gone from. Maybe we should go back to that other land we left behind that was the promised land that we were promised and that we had. Maybe we should go back there and learn to stay. . . .

"Stay? *Stay?* STAY?" the preacher choked.
"Rise ye up, we gotta get west.
This Pawnee pesterin's just a test.
I've done sent Jabal already to say
We're passin thru, we don't aim to stay.
You recollect how Sihon put up a fuss?
Being such a stubborn and ornery cuss?
Down at Jahaz he stood and fought
But his people were killed, his cattle were caught.
I don't think the Pawnees're that dern dumb.
Likely . . . that poundin is a medicine drum."

And Jesse S. went on before, dancing and rhyming, so that he looked a different man from what they thought. Or was he the same but they were different? They drew into themselves and clasped their own everlasting arms around their bodies and their own faces were their rocks of ages and their hearts hoped that they could abide with them a little longer. They didn't whistle anymore about the wide Mizzourye because they'd crossed it and it was just another muddy and was this the great beyond?

✳ His little sister was gone when Jabal came back that morning with the scout.

"Gone where?" he said.

"Just gone," his ma said hard-eyed. "I had her with me on the old horse and some Injuns took out after us and I was away from the rest and I was afraid the old horse couldn't make it to the rest, so I set her down where the grass and sage was the thickest and I said to her, 'Run, Dittany! Run and hide like you've seen the little buffalo calves do. Hide down deep as you kin in the ground with your head under your hands and me and Jesse S. will come back after you when the Injuns has rode away.' Then I kicked the old horse sharp and went off the other way. They follered me and I rode so hard the old horse liked to choke on his tongue. We got back to the others and the Injuns run off. Only when me and your pa went back to where I set her down, she wasn't there. We looked and looked for three days and your pa says we gotta get on."

"Show me where you set her down," Jabal said.

But his ma only looked back stony-faced and said, "I wisht I hadn't set her down. I hardly even knowed her. 'F I'd knowed the old horse could run so good, I coulda had her still."

157

Jabal went out alone to find his little sister who was the dog and gun and all the things he'd never had and always wanted. All the things he'd never owned. She was all the things. She was like a part of him because he'd raised her ever since their ma had dropped her without hardly noticing, being so tired of dropping young'uns like a cow. He had fed her with his own hands and taught her how to walk and talk and carried her under his arm most of the way to where they had come.

He took a fresh canteen of water and a blanket and some food and went out bitter in his head to find his little sister lying down in the grass like the little buffalo calves do hide.

But though he went up and down the land of sand and scrimpy grass and sage and watched the Injuns moving through the grass and rocks to see if they carried a little girl in a red calico shortgown with a cornhusk doll with a buckeye face and hands of whang, he did not find her. He stayed eight days so that more rains came down and two wagons passed him going east. He walked his horse over the vasty land but he did not find his little sister in the grass or her little doll.

The wagons went on without him finally. They called and whooed, but they had gotten so far ahead —he'd fallen so far behind. Jesse S. quit dancing long enough to hold a hurried prayer for the soul of his oldest boy. But his woman said she wished to God they'd never whistled their way across the wide Mizzourye and she was sorry for all the angry times against her young'uns who were thinning down in numbers and why hadn't she let the rocker chair fall into the fire those times when you couldn't see the moon.

Jabal wandered over the vasty land. And the more

suns and moons and stars that passed him up he had the feeling that he'd had so often in the past, the feeling that he was going to fly apart like black powder was inside him, the feeling that he was not going to be altogether and in one piece, the feeling that something was trying to get out.

twelve

When Rapaho woke and saw the snow falling against the buffalo robe he knew that something bad was going to happen. He knew by the snow. Snow was the end. Death of summer. Horror of winter. Empty eye of a spring which might not come.

"Hutch, you fool!" he said.

He called the mule and went to hunt the calf. It was down behind a boulder with its head drooping a little and its nose into the wind and it was coughing so that the little cover he'd made for it from one of the Navajo rugs was shaken free of snow.

He coaxed it to its feet and half-pulled and pushed it to the wagon. The calf which had been so fat and sleek and danced so on the hills was weak and sick.

But when he got the mule harnessed to the wagon and things slung in the wagon bed, he found he couldn't lift the calf into the wagon. He was too old. Too tired. Too weak. No matter how hard he tried, he could not lift it high enough, and the calf was too sick to walk.

He stood back and looked at the calf thru the snow. Blizzard snow. Quick tiny flakes. Just dots of white. But they clung to everything they touched and built so fast. When he looked away and out over the flat land he could see the air which had been so golden and so blue was white. Soon the cottonwood with the broken top was blotted out. Then the five cottonwoods. Then the whole plain. Then the boulders.

"We're never gonna make it out," he said.

He pulled the wagon up against a slope and tied the buffalo on the off side of it to make a flap that would be a doorway. He backed the mule and calf in between the wagon and the slope and tied them there. What wood was left and what old buffalo chips he'd been able to find, he piled under the wagon. It was not much of a shelter, but it would break the wind and they could have a small fire.

"Hutch you goddamned fool!" he kept saying with his mouth bittered.

He put the calf in between Berthy Conchita and him. The mule knew about blizzards. She had waited out many before. With the ponies. The mustangs. The old man. Blizzards and waiting them out were a part of life. Above the cry of the wind she thought she heard the drumming feet of the mustangs and she raised her head and made a noise in her throat.

The calf was lying down. Rapaho petted its thin little mane and felt its warmth against him.

"Little baby calf," he soothed it. "Daddy's baby calf . . . gonna be all right . . . promise . . . gonna be all right . . ."

So they sat that first day and night with the wind roaring around them and the little fire that was hardly more than a lick of a flame at their feet. The second night the calf was restless and kept rubbing at the Navajo cover. The mule kept raising her head and looking thru the dark at the calf. The calf kept stirring about. It was hearing the wind. It was remembering something it had never been told—Fol-

161

low the wind. Stand to the wind. String out and go against the wind.

While Rapaho slept that night it broke out of the shelter and stood to the wind. Rapaho crawled after it and pulled it back, though it kicked him some in the stomach and hurt him.

"Things is diff'runt," he told it. "You're daddy's baby calf now and we don't pay no attention to the wind. We don't foller it no more. You belong with your daddy and not out there with a herd that ain't. Just pay no attention."

But when it was day again he had to go out and rustle for more wood or chips. He tied a rope around the calf's neck and tied the other end to the mule's neck.

"Don't foller me," he told them. "I'll be right back."

He picked up his Big Fifty and wrapped the other Navajo rug around him. He pulled the black crepe that was going to be good for something sometime from his boot and tied it to the rifle barrel. He jammed the gun's butt down in the snow to be a marker for him. Then he turned back and called back to the mule and calf, "Don't worry now . . . stay put . . . even should you hear me yell out . . . stay where you are . . . Daddy'll be all right."

But when he stepped back and looked at his little rag of a flag whipping in the wind he could hardly see it. Everything was black and white in the sun that hadn't really come, but was hidden behind the mass of purple clouds. He might not find his way back. Not if he went far. What if he went too far and couldn't see the rag . . . if it should blow loose from the barrel . . . if he should fall and get his directions mixed . . . if . . .

"I'll be right back," he called again.

But still he hesitated seeing them standing there roped together with the snow slowly melting in the spring sun

162

and the wolves scratching away the snow which covered them and them helpless. Berthy Conchita would put up a fight because she knew about wolves. But what about the baby? What if . . .

And he found himself staring at the Big Fifty and thinking what they had killed together . . .

"We done wrong," he patted it roughly, "but no more."

He went out into the wind and snow at last and away from the shelter. But all he could find were a few pieces of wood so old it was almost dust in his hands and it had been by the trickle and was still damp. He did manage to rustle a little grass from under the snow for the calf and mule and he did find a few chips. But he didn't find enough of anything that he went for.

Still, the blizzard looked like it was letting up. The calf seemed better. If the wind would quit and the snow stop falling and the sun come out maybe he could axe a travois for the calf to lie on and they might make it out at that.

But when he got back to the shelter where the wind whipped the snow in a circle, he saw the mule standing alone and the rope that had tied her to the calf dragging over the ground.

thirteen

The calf lay on its side with its nose stretched out ahead of it into the wind it no longer felt. Its eyes were half open. But its legs were stiff. It was on its knees with its small head down as if just resting. It was in the sleeping pose.

Rapaho stopped and stared at it. He stopped a long way off and stared at it. He went closer, then stopped again. He circled it, coming down on it from the windward side at last. He did this to see if it would jump up, if it would move at all.

Course it won't, he told himself. It's just a little thing. It don't have no sentry bulls to tell it someone's comin. It don't yet know enough to jump and run.

"Sh . . . sh . . ." he called to it, "go."

But it stayed still with the snow laid over it like a blanket, standing out in big soft flakes on its coat. It was outlined in snow.

It knows bout snow, he told himself. It knows when they's snow to get down and get itself covered and it'll get warm. That's all the little thing's done. It's just got itself warm.

He came nearer, his boots cracking the snow.

"It's me," he called out finally. "Crissake . . . it's me, your daddy. You kin get up now. You kin run now. It's only your daddy. Don't be afraid."

But it never moved. He stopped again and waited. His eyes squinted hard to make out any movement of the snow over the calf. To see if the snow went up and down, if it was breathing snow over a live animal. But there was not even a tiny frost cloud above the head of the calf. The frost cloud that should have been above the head of the calf, it was not there.

"Looky . . . it's me. . . ."

Then for a time he stood where he was. The calf stayed where it was. The stars, too. Only the wind moved. And then some snow jumped up and ran over the ground like a live thing. The snow, it was alive.

"It's dead," he said.

When he said that, there was nothing more to say.

Two or three stars fell.

He walked up to it then. He stared down at it. The snow did not move, save when the wind touched it. He knelt, brushed some of the snow back from its eyes, leaned down till his lashes touched its lashes.

"This ain't my calf," he said, drawing back his hand.

He shivered hard. This was some other little calf. This poor thing, this mangy thing with its roughened coat and spindly legs and ragged hoofs. This poor thing, it was not his.

His heart began to beat very hard. It choked him the way it beat. It hurt, too. He held his chest hard with his arms to keep his heart from jumping out of it. The snow was covered with purple spots. Also the sky. The whole world. Then the pain slipped down out of his throat and he felt better and raised his head and looked to the west where the land rolled up against the sky and crowded it.

"Yes," he said, "he's up there. Where the valleys are gettin green under the snow and where they's a herd he can run with and it's warmer than common because the wind don't get down in them valleys. He's where it's warm. This poor little thing," he looked back down at the spike of a calf, "likely it lost its mama. It got losted from the herd and strayed. The wolves probably scared it, howlin and follerin after it. Them damn wolves . . . why is it they always have the strength to foller? Why is it they never give up? They ain't half as big as one tiny calf, yet somethin gives em the strength. . . ."

He patted the little calf on its thin hump. Brushed at the snow and patted it some more.

"Likely your mama is lookin for you even now," he told it. "If I see her, I'll tell her. I'll tell her it come quick, dyin, and that you never, no not even once, felt it. I'll tell her how you was laid out so nice right like you was sleepin, like she taught you, and there wasn't no wolves round botherin you nor tryin to eat you. . . ."

He heaped snow over its eyes now, and over the hump. Then he began crawling around it and heaping more on, like a dog.

"No one'll get you if I cover you good," he said. "Buzzards don't really know when things is dead. They can't really tell. It's just a guess on their part and if you're covered real good, they'll just take you for a boulder or a hill they never happened to notice before."

After he covered the calf, he still knelt beside it, thinking how warm it was in there now and how nothing would get to it. He was pleased that he had thought to cover the calf even though it wasn't his.

"That's the ways folks are who have young'uns of their own," he said. "They take care of anyone's young'uns cause they understand—well, all folks feel the same toward all young'uns," he finally decided.

166

He stood up and brushed the snow from his leggings. Beat his hands to warm them. Sighed an old man sigh.

Then he heard the *rattle rattle rattle* of the dried hoofs he'd tied round Berthy Conchita's neck to keep wolves from her, and he waited, without turning, for her to come up with him. When he thought she was almost to his shoulder he said, "Looky here, Berthy . . . a little old calf . . . dead."

The mule stopped and looked down at the heap of snow. She snuffled at it. Pawed at it with her front hoof.

"Quit now," he said. "You'll undo all the good I've done."

He slapped her leg to push her back, but still she nuzzled at the snow and blew into it.

"Quit, you consarned mule," he said.

And then she began to rumble down deep in her throat.

"Quit takin on," he said. "It's not anyone we ever knowed. Just a little losted calf."

But the mule still pawed at the snow, and then he saw the bit of Navajo rug fluttering its edge.

"Whereat did you get that?" he asked the pile of snow with his heart starting to knot up in his throat. "That wasn't yours. That was Crissake's. It ain't right to steal. It ain't . . . but . . . couldn't be . . ."

But at last he knew it was.

He sat down carefully by the mound of snow. He began to uncover the calf. Patted its hump. Rubbed its legs. Brushed the snow off its eyes.

"My little baby calf," he kept saying, and sometimes he would say, "Why didn't you come when I called? How come you didn't jump up when I called? How come you went away and died . . . away from me? How come?"

The wind was full of teeth. They chewed at his throat and he didn't care.

fourteen

"I wanted you to see the flowers," he said at last. "It ain't fair that you never got to see the flowers."

The snow had begun falling again, and now it fell on his open hands. He looked down at the flakes and saw how slowly they melted.

"They're mostly in the spring," he said. "Round Plum Crick."

He didn't know the names of any of the flowers. Not even their Injun names. That was because before—before the calf—he had never really noticed them, except as sometimes being and sometimes not.

"Some are white," he said, "some blue, some red. Some have long throats and you can look way down into them. Sometimes there's a bug down there. Just walkin round. Sometimes he looks up and waves at you. Other flowers have chokey throats and you see their throats right off because they're right on top. And they's others that are broad across like a big open mouth, but when you get down close it ain't no open mouth at all, because they's millions and millions of little tiny eyes down there. The eyes are yellow. Well, sometimes green."

He cleared his throat and stared down at the snow-

168

flakes. But he had not said all that he must say about the flowers. There would be no other time to tell about them. He thought hard.

"Some grow on long stems and stand up above the buffalo grass. I guess even the buffalo eat em. Antelope, too. But not the wolves. Nor buzzards. Probably bugs eat em, though. And them that don't stand up high, they're either in little bushy plants or layin out in vines that twist all thru the grass. They just pop out when the wind blows . . . when it pushes em so they show . . . then they pop out and look to see what they is to see. They don't get eaten so much, cause they're protected down against the ground. They get stepped on, but not eaten. It's better to just get stepped on . . . maybe be a little bruised . . . but still go on livin."

He looked at the white and black night around him and wondered where they'd all gone, the flowers.

"And you never got to see the rivers," he said. "Oh, Platte, Niobrara . . . but them ain't all . . . they's rivers and they's rivers."

He looked far beyond the mound of snow and saw them all. He knew them all. Their names rang thru his mind like bells or wild geese calling.

"They's Bear-in-the-Lodge . . . Snake . . . Wind River . . . Black Thunder . . . Old Woman . . Greybull . . . Poison Spider . . . Medicine Bow . . . I could name you a hunderd and a hunderd hunderd and you'd never be able to tell em all back to me."

He laid one hand on the mound of snow and he could feel the calf's dark nose beneath it.

"They's so many," he said softly. "And you never got to see em run. Never got to see em twist down no canyon. Spill over no ford. Carry away the big cottonwoods like they was little straws of dried grass stems. No, you never.

169

"You never got to see nothin," he said.

The snow began blowing in his face. It was coming head on. It clung to his beard and he could see it on his eyebrows even looking down. His hair was so heavy with the snow it didn't blow anymore, but hung wet and wretched down his back, and one long piece of it was stuck to his throat where it dripped water down into his collar to fall on his chest.

"We coulda had such a good time," he said wistfully. "We could a gone on and on. We woulda met lots of nice people and they would all have said, 'Oh, looky there . . . that man's got him a buffalo calf and ain't it purty!'"

He smiled, seeing how they would have gone on and on.

"Yes, that's what they woulda said. They would all have stood in the streets to watch us pass by. Even on hot days. Even on days when the sun is slammin the dust down flat. Even on days when they ain't a breath of air that ain't fire and blood red air, they woulda come out of the saloons, the shops, the stables, and they woulda said . . . Ain't that the finest calf you ever seen? They would watch us pass by and they might even have liked us. Well, of course," he said quickly, "they woulda liked *you*. But I mean, me, too. They might have liked me, too. Since Haggis and Chien and Joner died . . . ain't nobody liked me, but you. And, far as that goes . . . it wasn't no credit to be liked by *them*. It wasn't as if they amounted to anything themselves. They was just like me . . . not   much   good."

The wind came around him cold. Against his mouth cold. Even his tongue was cold.

"We might even have gone somewhere on a train," he said. "You cain't never tell. We might have got to ride on one of them. Maybe even for free. We coulda gone every-

170

where . . . all across the whole land without walking even one tiny little step. No sweatin. No joggin. No runnin. No tirin. No wantin for water. No worryin bout wind . . . sun . . . nothin. Just settin and ridin and maybe bowin to folks as we passed em by. Maybe yellin at the emergrants as we passed em by. Maybe even feelin sorry for them as we passed em by.

"And I woulda made a fine silver bridle for you to wear and put stones in . . . turquoise stones from the Mexican mines . . . blue stones to match your feet . . . and maybe little brass circles danglin and clinkin in your mane . . . and maybe some kind of white, fine, soft, handweaved robe to throw over you and it with beads stitched all over."

He smiled, seeing the calf in its fine robe and brass circlets and silver bridle. He changed the picture so that he, too, wore fine clothes. White men's clothes, not fringed leggings and the old stained jacket.

"I'd likely have to shave my beard off," he said. "I'd have to take a bath and clean up a little. Pare my nails down even. Maybe comb my eyebrows a little. Wouldn't do to ride on a train without bein cleaned up some.

"On a train," he said, "we woulda set across from each other. Or maybe side by side." He frowned. He'd never really seen inside a train. Not a real look inside. Just a peep and that a casual I-ain't-doin-nothin-to-your-damned-old-train-you-dumb-engineer look. But he thought you could sit either way.

"Hear the whistle blowin?" he said. "We might even get to blow it, however it is that you do it. Course we'd have to wait to be asked, and then we'd have to see how it was done and not pull or push or jerk the wrong thing . . . but we shouldn't ask how it's done . . . it wouldn't look right

171

for a man and a buffalo calf travelin across the country together not to know how to blow a whistle. We wouldn't
want to look ignorant."

He nodded and pushed his beard down farther against
his chest.

"Hear the whistle blow?" he said again. "Hear it
whooooooo? Jreeeek . . . Jreeeek . . . Jreeeek . . . that's how
it goes. *Jreek, Jreek* and we'd scare the antelopes. Antelopes scare easy. Course, we wouldn't want to scare em so
they're really scared. Just so's they'd jump up and run a little and then look back. Not so's they jump up and run and
maybe break a leg. Specially some little tiny baby antelope."

He felt better that they had not actually scared the antelopes too much and he saw them standing off to one side
of the train just ready to run if need be. Just looking at the
train with their long eyes and the sun so pretty on their
coats and their legs so pointy and their rumps so polished.
Then he saw the antelopes move as in a dream, leap
slowly in the air and all the plain was empty and he was
satisfied that none were scared and none were hurt and no
babies were left behind with broken legs, and he and the
calf went on in the train with it *whoooooing* and scaring
the settlers in the night.

"Their damn bobwire," he said. "By hell, we'd scare em!
We'd get em out of their beds and on their feets with no
boots because they put up that damn bobwire that cuts
animals across their chests and legs when they're runnin.
We'd scare the hell out of them in their muddy little sod
houses and their dirty little shacks that wouldn't hold back
a cup of water on the roof. We'd watch their eyes get big
and hear em whisperin back and forth, 'What's *that?*' and
watch em sweat till they was standin in a pool of sweat

172

cause while the train was *whooooin* we'd be howlin like Cheyenne. And then we'd get on past em a laughin and a hangin onto the whistle and *jreek jreek* . . . them and their damn bobwire and *jreek jreek* . . . them and their damn bean patches and *jreek jreek*." He paused, then added, "Settlers is men and women and they can take care of theirselves and be scared and it serves em right for bein where they ain't wanted . . . but not little animals . . . they need someone to look after them and say it's all right."

The mule was getting restless, rustling in the snow for a mouthful of grass, rattling her dried hoofs.

"You ought to show more respect and listen quiet," he said to her. "You know bout bobwire."

But she didn't even lift her head.

"We'd go up in the mountains," he went on to the calf, "even where they's green medders that no man has ever seen and you know what I bet? I bet that up there in them medders we might find some of your folks. Yessir . . . they's prob'ly up there . . . holed up somewhere . . . hidin out. And if we seen em as we went by we wouldn't poke some feller aside of us and say, Looky there, buffalo! We wouldn't, cause like as not he'd pull out a Big Fifty and blast away. It might even be your own ma that he killed. Yes, she might still be runnin somewhere and he might kill her. And how would she feel seein the gun bringin her down and her own baby calf sittin right there in the winder with its nose pushed against the glass and watchin it all? Why, she'd think you done it.

"And when we was done," he leaned closer to the mound of snow so that both his hands were on it. "When we was done runnin over the country on them trains, then we'd go to a ranch somewheres . . . we'd find us a little ranch somewheres with lots and lots of trees round it and a nice stream without no name (we'd name it after you) and then we'd settle there. Down where winter never comes and the sun is always warm but never hot. Where it's the promised land. Where it's peace. Quiet. Birds singin. We wouldn't let nothin else come along and sing but birds. No drums. No flutes. Maybe a church bell could ring. Yes, a church bell somewhere nearby and we would watch the people goin to church on Sunday, comin across the plain in their hats and bonnets and we might even go ourselves and sit in the back. Just to listen. Just to see what it was like that everyone went.

"We'd go into town sometimes and buy flour and beans and coffee. But no bullets. And we'd have folks in to visit sometimes, because they'd all want to come and see you and we'd have to have a sign painted up that said, HERE LIVES THE ONLY TAMED BUFFALO CALF IN THE WORLD WITH HIS PA. Yes, we should put that about the pa on the sign so people would know better than to try to steal you in the nights, because it would mean that I'd just have to kill em and I don't want to kill nothin nor no one no more.

"And then when I was a real real real old man and you was a real real real old bull, we'd die. Maybe together. I wouldn't go and die ahead of you. I couldn't die ahead of you and leave you. No, you shouldn't fret about that. I'd see you died first and I'd bury you real grand with flowers on your grave, planted flowers so they'd keep comin back each spring. And maybe, by that time, I'd have a friend that I could trust and he'd take over the place and look after where we was both buried side by side and wouldn't nobody ever come along and dig like dogs and say, 'Looky here . . . I found me a buffalo skull . . . some Injun must've buried it.' Or, 'Looky here . . . I found me a old man.' Wouldn't nobody ever separate us.

174

"But you didn't wait," he said.

He pressed his face against the mound of snow and felt the snow coming in thru his lashes.

"You didn't wait. You didn't wait for the flowers or the train ride or the ranch. You went on ahead of me too fast and what'll I do without you when the flowers come and the trains call and they ain't no one but me?"

He sat back. The stars were hard. The white cold lay over everything. The sky was very high. There was a moon coming on.

"It's gonna freeze tonight," he said. "Gonna freeze hard."

But Rapaho and the mule had taken only a few steps when he turned back to the snow mound, ripped the eagle claw from his ear so that blood was sprinkled on the snow, and pressed it into the hump of the calf.

"This'll mark it," he called out to the listening world. "This red-tipped eagle claw will be a mark and a sign unto you. I say, a sign unto you is given. Praised be the name of the calf."

fifteen

The Cheyenne drum was calling him. The flutes were playing in his head. A Blackfoot whistle had started up five days ago. Now he sat by his fire on the sheltered side of the wagon, humming to the flutes and whistle and sometimes talking to the drum. He was no longer afraid of them. No, they had become as friends who understood him. And as he did with things, he had named them. He'd given them the names of his old dead friends Haggis, Chien and Joner, who were not good men, because he thought these things were not good either.

The sky was changing from blue to black again, and he watched it. There was nothing new in what it did. It was always going from one to the other, and sometimes going from blue to red or gold or grey. He had seen it all his life. He had watched it how many times . . . would a man say hundreds and hundreds . . . or would he say thousands? Yes, thousands, he thought, and thousand thousands and words that were numbers even beyond those.

Even when drinking, when gambling, hunting, all his life he had never missed seeing it go from blue to black. It was the one thing he had done all on his own and it was no little thing, no matter what another person might think. It was no little thing to throw down a winning hand and go outside and watch it turn from blue to black. It was no little thing to let a herd pass and feel the barrel colding in his hands and turn his nose from the smell of blood to the smell of night coming on.

And, as usual, when it turned from blue to black, he found a star. Not the evening star. There was always a littler one somewhere high where the sky looked thin. It wasn't as big or as bright or as showy as the evening star, but he could always find it and he liked it better because it was brave enough to try to outshine the evening star when it knew it had no place in the sky beside it, beside its enemy who wished all eyes of men to be on it. But, he thought, something kept it where the evening star could never pull it down. That was the way things were, he thought. There was some order. A certain way of things being held to certain places so that trees didn't walk around and rocks didn't run and mountains didn't fall down flat. Now he cut his eyes at the evening star. Such a show-off it always seemed. "Looky at me!" it always said, and he stuck his tongue out at it and waved his hand at it for it to go away and yelled, "You ain't so much . . . you ain't as bright as my fire."

And, as usual, the others came on then. They came like they were being pushed thru the sky by something behind them. They came like wolves ringing something dying, yet it was strong enough to fight, and they sat on their haunches which were always cold (you could tell by their color they were icy cold) and they watched and they waited. And after a while they all moved off westerly still sitting. That had always been a puzzle to him, how they moved without getting up on their feet and running. It made him wonder, after years and years of studying wolves, if maybe it was

177

the world which moved and not the sky, and the stars only looked to be moving.

"Well," he said to them, "here we are together again."

And they flicked their ears at him and wriggled hard, Yes, here we are. . . .

Later on the moon got up. An old moon. Chewed and showing scars of age and each night's battle with the shadow of the earth, it got up, somewhat drunk, he thought, and wobbled across the sky.

"Now the moon has got more freedom than the stars," he said, "and why . . . and why . . . and why?"

So much for the moon and, "Howdy, moon," he said and tossed it a salute, a nice salute like he had learned when he was with the Dragoons.

A coyote barked to his right, or was it his left? His ears weren't so good for hearing outside things anymore being so full of Cheyenne drums and flutes and whistles. He listened hard and it barked again, and he called to it and smiled and thought, He's just beyond my feets, somewhere down on the flats. And he liked to hear it and wanted it to go on and it did and barked three times quick and broke off with a whine that made him kind of chill and sigh and also a little unhappy because it brought back so many nights.

Cheyenne nights and raids. Horses hoofs, stolen horses heaving hard with his hand on the leather thong around their necks and the sweat from the horses and the foam from their mouths running down his fingers, slickering them and warming them when it was cold. Colors in the nights. Colors in flashes. Fires and brown legs and backs and red. Red of headdresses and blankets and beads and even eyes. Red eyes. Sleepless tired eyes. Drunken eyes. A lot of red in the nights' black. Red in dancehall skirts and dancehall slippers and dancing beads that swung between breasts and caught in the clefts and bounced free again and even red lace to match red lips and red cheeks and red red hair. Red of the cards and red of the hacienda and red of the flowers that grew there by themselves and red of the rooster's comb which pranced thru the court and red of the whole damn big world, he thought, winding it up.

And everywhere a man went there were coyotes breaking off their third bark with a wail and making him sad even in someone's arms. Coyotes were death, he decided. They were death to good things, always crying words that were not human words, but that he felt and could translate to himself but not to another human or even to the mule. They meant hardship and pain and misery and all the bad things. Yet when you had the good things, the coyotes' words made you hold onto them even tighter and made you care for them more because you knew the coyotes were telling you how they were coming and bringing all the bad of the world with them . . . and they didn't lie. Someday . . . you thought . . . someday . . . someplace . . . sometime . . . sure they'll come.

"We are very very old, Mr. Rapaho," he said suddenly. And then: "I think little coyote . . . maybe this is the time."

He hadn't been thinking it, but as soon as he said it, he knew it was true, for there were strange sounds from the sky and the earth shook and the wind began to blow.

It was a dead cold wind. It came in single file. It blew down from where the north had been stretched over the empty place. Where the earth hung upon nothing.

It smelled like gunsmoke, blood, hides, sweat, beer, sawdust, cheap perfume.

It chinked like spurs, triggers, Cheyenne rattles, pony beads, rhinestone garters, earrings, piano keys scraping up and down, bottles, shattered mirrors, bullets, boots of a

179

hanging man. Also like the lamp swinging from the adobe ceiling of Spanish Bean John's down at Santa Fe where harlots, hunters, every kind of wanderer tied bracelets, bangles, buttons, things they thought were lucky and would bring them back someday. It also cussed real good in Spanish, Cheyenne, Kiowa, Pawnee, Kaintuck and Texas tongues. It hurrahed and tittered too.

But it had a taste that was bitter like a wallow where dead men had been drinking.

It carried a whole world of rags, rubble, filth. Fringed jackets flapped past. Eagle feathers, stringy scalps, buffalo wool, splintered wagon tongues, bloody cavalry gloves, silver-hilted Spanish skinning knives wrapped with colored thread, slick and shiny harlots' quilts. Also whole wagons covered with green mold. Injun villages, all kinds. Sickly yellow lanterns of the tent town. Hunks of silver, copper, gold. Embroidered *God Bless* mottos of godless places. Peeling signs such as IF YOU'RE LOOKIN FOR TOMB-STONE, TURN AROUND—THIS AIN'T IT. Cattle towns with boardwalks where the sun and moon were only a couple of blobs to be shot at drunkenly as they rose behind the heap of manure at the livery stable and set behind the heap of buffalo bones waiting for the train to take them east.

Rapaho turned away from the wind and toward the Dancehall Girls and O'Ryan, then toward Arky. But none of them were there.

"Likely, you couldn't help me nohow," he said.

When the wind hit the world where Rapaho sat, it became only a wind again. Once it touched dirt, it was only a wind. It did not glitter and it smelled of earth. It had no taste. It said nothing. Where it hit there were no trees for it to moan against. There was nothing it could make scrape, such as a bush. Rocks do not scrape.

180

Rapaho got up then and faced it in its eye.

"You're from The Salt, I reckon," he said.

Black buzzards rode sitting on the wind. From the down side of the brim of his hat, they rode in on the wind. They were big. Broad-winged. Their feathers dripped below them. The whole western and the northern sky was filled with them, making a black cloud.

Rapaho watched them coming on. It was then his head began to hurt. They seemed to be flying against his eyes and their dripping wings became his lashes beating against the greyness of his eyes. But beating faintly, as a moth might beat. Yet he was not afraid, but only hurt. In his head. Around his eyes. Under his throat.

Where they passed over their tail feathers cut long grooves in the ground. He saw the grooves were old trails which had been hidden. Spanish trails with Spanish armor lying beside, the gold of the dented breastplates dull in the dim moonlight. Injun trails with broken bowls beside and basket and string bags and mashed beads. Animal trails where bones and horns and hoofs lay still, yet the imprint of the hoofs was still moving thru the dust. Where the hoofs which were not there were walking, he could see their marks.

And then the grooves went deeper and dead Injuns, dead cattle, dead drovers, dead hunters, dead immigrants . . . the died-of-old-age dead and the died-by-killing dead stood up.

"Yep . . . you're from The Salt."

He began to tug at his jacket and the yellow scarf and floppy hat to take them off and hide like always. But then he thought, I ain't gonna need em no more. And so he smoothed his jacket front and patted at the scarf and took off the hat, brushed fondly at it raggedness, clucked his tongue a little when he saw the brim was tearing away

181

from the crown, licked one finger and crimped the tattered feathers, shined the gold coin with his thumb and carefully put on the hat again after pulling his hair down neatly over his shoulders so that it fell like a cape.

"I'm ready now, I reckon."

But then he thought of the Big Fifty (and it was a good old gun) and the Spanish skinning knives (none better ever skinned a man) and the coffee pot (not worth much but just got old enough to make good coffee). And he went on and thought about the little bag of gold dust that he carried up under the seat and his other pair of boots and what was left of the beans and flour and his blanket and the robe. And then he thought some more, and there was the doll, the little doll that had been his special charm and that he'd lugged from one end of the world he knew to the other.

Tenderly he took out the velvet box that held the skinning knives and doll and laid them on the seat with the gold dust set on top. Over it all he laid his Big Fifty for the last time.

With every minute he was weaker now. The sky was coming and going. Also the wind. The ground. Now he hurried quick as his old hip would let him, and when it caught as he clambered down from the wagon he looked at it and said, "That's the last time for you!"

From the fire he took a piece of burned wood and on the wagon side he wrote the best he could a note for the man he knew would find it: HAPY BIRF DAY.

Then he chuckled, went back to the fire and picked up a dead branch he had meant to burn. But he wanted it now only to hold. It did not seem right to wait for what was coming just standing like a tree and holding nothing. All his life he had been holding something, a Cheyenne lance, a whip, a knife, his Big Fifty.

"Oh, they was things and things," he said.

182

His eyes fell on Berthy Conchita. Old like him. Nose all grey. Rustling in the snow. Hoping . . . a little grass. He found a stone and threw at her. Yelled. Drove her off limping a little, hurting a little on one shoulder from the stone. Looking back sometimes. Stopping. But then going on.

"Go along now," he yelled at her, "tain't fittin you should be here when they come."

Then he raised his piece of deadwood like a standard, grinned, but his old tooth began to ache.

"Well," he said to the tooth, "looks like we both got used up at the same time."

The buzzards passed over.

"Mr. Rapaho," he said, "did you ever stop to think of where it is we came from or where it is we're goin?" "No, I never," he answered himself, "but I reckon now might be a pretty good time." "Well, Mr. Rapaho, do you remember when it was that we come bustin out into this?" "That I do." "Well, Mr. Rapaho . . . reckon we go back there . . . or where?" "Now   that   I   couldn't say. But I kinda think that if you wait a minute or two more, we'll know."

The wind turned darker than the sky. The stars smoked out. Even the moon. Now thru the smoke came eagles, nighthawks, and butterflies. All colors, all shapes and sizes they were and they themselves were words written against the sky.

<pre>
              up   your
        you   my   me   little
   rise   dearest   give to   hand
                            and
</pre>

PROMISED

```
      went out on a went out on a went out
      fox                                    wintery
           prayed for the moon to give him
      the                                    night
      and                                    light
        he                                   him
```

LAND

```
for    he'd    many    a    mile    to    go    that
                            night
```

PROMISED LAND

before he reached the town-o the town-o

Squinting hard and biting his tongue he managed to spell out *you, hand, fox,* and *land,* and that was enough. He knew what it said.

The moon began to boom and boom and he felt better because it was the old moon back from wherever it had gone and, "Howdy moon," he waved his standard, "thought that was you before, but wasn't sure, and where you been?" The Cheyenne drum was chanting *Rapaho-o-o-o-o-o.* The flutes were whirring with the smoke. The stars were dancing in the snow. The Blackfoot whistle whined and whined.

Then he heard a rumble. A steady rocking rumble. A quivering and quaking. A sudden deep-earth shaking. And he strained to see them come.

"Well, Hutch," he said, "take keer you goddam fool. It's a pure shame you never knowed that it was me that answered prayers you said and paid your debts. Mine woulda been wrote off, but you had to go and meddle, you had to turn me in. You're gonna be mighty surprised at how much I owe."

Red lightning flashed behind the smoke of sky and he straightened now as much as his bent back would let him.

184

Lifted his head. Pushed back his hat. Pulled some of the blowing hair from the corner of his mouth. Waved once vaguely to the Dancehall Girls, O'Ryan and old Arky.

"Well, Hutch," he said, "you winned out over me at last. You got it all . . . last old loose tooth and all. But all the good's gone out of it."

He threw the standard down and braced himself with shaky knees. For they were coming. Driven by the dead ciboleros from The Salt. And there were Injun hunters too. Hide men. Haggis and Chien and Joner. All of them were coming for the last cibolero left on earth. He saw a flash of bone, of horns like stars, of golden hoofs and humps made of red velvet. And then the diamond eyes . . .

He moved toward them feebly, grinning, waving an I-am-here. For didn't he know what was coming?

The sound stopped all at once. There were no more eagle-nighthawk-butterfly words in the sky. Nor was there any rumble of hoofs nor rattle of ciboleros. No Cheyenne drum. No flutes. No whistle. Only the stars dropping by the dying fire. Only the clean black sky. The silent moon.

It was quiet at last and there was no sound in all the world.

Down on the knob below, the mule turned back to look at where the old man stood. She wondered why was he so quiet. Why was he so quiet? She rustled for a shaft of grass she saw sticking up in the hard cold moonlight. She chomped on the grass. Looked back at the old man. He still stood silhouetted against the sky. Fixed.

She nickered in her chest. Still he didn't move. She rubbed her nose over the slight bruise the rock had made. She knew where there was some better grass. But she wanted the old man to walk her there. It was a lonely trip past coyotes.

✱ Rain was falling in the shallow river. Little holes appeared where the drops hit and went away so quick. Across the river there was a haze of rain standing up blue beyond the short grass. The boy sitting on the old horse began to feel chilly. The rain was soaking into his skin and dripping off his hair onto his neckbone.

Inside his shirt he carried a little doll. It was made of cornhusks and buckeyes and had whang hands that had little flowers withered in them. It had once had cornsilk hair. But even the doll had been scalped like the little girl that he had found.

She lay across his saddle wrapped in his jacket. She lay on her belly and was so small that just the tips of her fingers and the ends of her toes stuck out from under the jacket.

He had passed the warriors earlier that morning and hidden from them down in the river where an island with a scattering of cottonwoods gave a pale shelter. The warriors were carrying loot that looked like white man's loot. They were carrying dresses, blankets, boots, kettles, even guns. One had a woman's bonnet on. Another had an apron tied round his shoulders against the rain.

For a while he had gone the way he'd seen them

come. It was easy to follow their trail by the things they'd dropped. A broken keg of rum. A bucket of pitch. A trail of flour from a flour barrel they'd tried to lasso and drag.

He finally crossed the river and went west by north. After a while it quit raining and the sun came out. Also the buzzards and the hawks. They followed him. And up ahead there were more just circling. They made a lot of shadows over the ground.

He reined the old horse on the top of a shallow hill and looked down into the narrow valley. Down there was the wagon train. All in pieces and smouldering a little. The plain became very hot. It was already very quiet except for the sound of the birds.

He left the horse and walked down to the wagons. He looked at all the dead men. Then he looked at all the women. And there were some young'uns too. All were dead. The horses driven off. The oxen shot. What was any good was gone.

He went back up the hill after taking with him a bucket of pitch and a piece of wood that was not quite burned through. He scraped out a grave on the hill and buried the little girl in it. With the piece of wood for a marker he wrote with a stick dipped in pitch, LITLE PUP FROM BURND WAGGINS.

When he was done he saw that he still had the doll in his shirt so he decided to keep it for luck. Jabal had seen it first, but when he started to jump down from the old horse to see it closer, he had stopped. In mid-air he had stopped. Like he was dead he had stopped. And it was him, this other one, this one without a name that no one knew about who had stepped down to the ground.

He wiped his hands on his leather leggings.

"Well, Jabal," he said, "this is the Promised Land that *you* was promised but that *I* got."

While he was standing there he was taken by four Pawnees slipping up behind. But this one was strong. This one was mean. This one was not afraid. And two months later when he ran off from the Pawnee camp and went to live with the Cheyenne and they asked what was his name he said, "Why . . . I call myself Rapaho."

sixteen Suddenly Hutch was standing there.

Suddenly Hutch was standing there and it was night and there was a moon that jumped in and out between clouds running wild.

Suddenly Hutch was standing there and a train was whistling down on the flats below that it was going to see the world. People. Tall wood houses. Brick-paved streets. Fiddles and rocking chairs. Bits of fence and flowers. Mountains with the ever snow. Rivers with no names. Cities burning. Balconies of iron. Ships with sails. Merchants, rich men, generals and kings.

I am standin where?

His head was dazey. Everything about him floated away then toward him like a thick wet fog. The wind tasted strange in his mouth. The ground walked up and down under his feet and he clung to it with his toes.

All the strangeness stopped at once when he saw the hunter's wagon with its feathers tossing a little in the night wind, the embers of the fire going down and down, the battered coffee pot slung beside it on a rock, the old boots with the toes curled up, the Navajo rug crumpled as if someone had just got up from underneath it, the hunk of bacon dropped by one wheel, the open bag of beans dribbling over the side of the wagon bed and falling one by one with no sound, only making small dents in the snow.

Something had just happened and it was over. He had missed it. Come too late. But he could feel it in his hands, in the palms of his hands it was there still. Also in the wind. In the blades of grass beneath the snow. Even the rocks knew what it was had happened.

I was at the fort . . . and I was saying . . . "Scuse me" . . . and had that poster in my hand . . . "and but I think . . . maybe I orter turn him in . . . and if the three hunderd is still to be got for him . . . course even if it ain't . . . there was these nesters and I owed them three dollars and they got burned out. . . all the way burned out . . . them too . . . helped to bury em you know . . . found this eagle claw . . . had this poster . . . bounty hunter come last year said he wasn't no good . . . thought maybe . . . though it ain't the kinda thing I wanta do . . ."

That was all he could remember. Except for the flag flying from a post in the middle of a square place of ground and horses whisking their tails as they passed by and the sun so bright on the captain's yellow kerchief and a lady walking with her skirt pulled to one side and a parasol she carried making her look tall and someone yelling *Hoooo-OOOOOoooooo* and tamed Injuns wrapped in blankets, beads, rags, hats, sitting with their begging bowls and lice and a pony painted above the double wooden gates and lots of feet in boots stomping smartly up and down so that the knees above the boots clicked and snow . . . snow . . . snow beginning to fall down thru the sun rays . . .

I was down there and I turned him in and what am I doin here?

He began to be afraid.

The captain said he was an ornery old cuss . . . bad, that

190

was the word . . . and had been knowed to kill . . . and he usta know him when he was a young Dragoon . . . and they always thought he shot some man workin a telegraph key when he kept station for the Pony Express . . . and also out in . . . and up by . . . and I turned him in with that old poster tearin in the wind and his name black acrost it.

So what am I doin here where he kin kill me?

He crouched behind a boulder then and stared around the camp which was bright, then black, as the moonlight came and went with each sickly cloud. But the camp remained the same. The fire going down and down. The Navajo rug turned back in rumples. The coffee pot . . . the boots . . . the beans . . .

Reckon already they come and got him? Beat   me back? How could they beat me back? But maybe they could . . . was ridin Scoggins' old plow horse cause I couldna find the mule . . . and it went lame . . . but if they rode real hard and quick . . . right off . . . right after I said about the poster and his wagon and the eagle claw . . . yeah . . . they   coulda   beat   me   back.

He chewed his lip.

Only why don't I remember it?

He crouched down lower so that even his head was hidden and studied the rock with his fingers and tried to go back and remember.

Gotta remember and go back . . . cause if they ain't come and fetched him off he's round right close . . . jump me . . . don't wanta die.

The train whistled farther off and spooked something and he could hear their hoofs rumbling in the earth and when he put his ear to the rock he could hear them louder. But when it was silent again he lifted his head and stared again at the wagon where the moon was so bright for an

191

instant that he could see the red paint on the shafts and something written on the side.

It's awful to be old and keep forgettin.

An owl came down low and he could hear its wings as it passed over.

They ain't no horse or mule that would be his . . . cause I don't see any. So they prob'ly got him and put him on his horse or mule and took him off. Bet   that's   what happened. Bet that's what it was. They come right quick togethim   cause the captain said   well, he didn't say   butwhenItoldhim   he   looked   like they'd   come   right quick. Kinda rustled his feet and that prob'ly meant that they were gonna come and so they must've prob'ly come and cause I've been so tired and worried   about that three dollars   and them gettin killed   and the damn windowglass and all and no Dittany come in either this year   guess I slept on the horse all the way back and   that's   why I   don't remember.

After a long time, after the thundering had gone out of the ground and been forgotten by the rock and the train whistled so far away that men he didn't even know heard it and waved to it from horseback, he got up from behind the boulder with a pain in his back and a catching in his hip and went carefully toward the wagon. He stopped twenty feet from it and stared at it. It seemed to be moving toward him but it stopped as the moonlight came again and the wind dropped the feathers.

Reckon I orter go down to home, he thought. Shouldna even come up here. They might be there waitin. . . . Course even if they fetched the money with em don't think I could take it in my hand and say Thank you sir and him a standin there with handcuffs on or lookin down at me from his horse's or his mule's back. He was so old . . . older'n me . . . and just out huntin and then I come along . . .

But he took another step toward the wagon. There were never any sounds, save the wind. The faint whisper of snow as it sifted down from the seat sometimes. Once a coyote. Nothing else.

He really is gone. They come and got him. And I ain't no right to be here . . . here with another man's treasures . . . things he wouldn't want no one else to touch like I wouldna want no one a fingerin over my velvet chairs or the harpsichord or M. Gruber's trunk and he was camped up here all this time and I been to town and to the nesters three times and to the fort and he coulda come right down to my place and stripped it clean. But he never. Never even looked inside that I know of. He was a   bad   old   man . . . an outlaw . . . Wanted even . . . and it don't seem right that if he didn't come stealin and pokin at my stuff that I should come up here now stealin and pokin at his stuff.

He was almost to the wagon now.

Course . . . if he is gone then it's same as the Conestoga Graveyard . . . I mean he ain't comin back for it likely . . . and if there might be some things he'd like to have looked after special so the snow and dust don't get em and the rains, come spring . . .

He shifted his weight and sighed.

Reckon if someone come and took me off   I'd want someone to look after what I got. When I thought I' was   goin   off   to   jail   I was gonna ask Scoggins . . . and it is the same sorta . . . cause he don't know who it was that turned him in and even if he does and has been in my house when I was gone then he knows how good I look after things and since we're both old men an all . . . think he'd be glad . . .

193

He took the last step to the wagon and then stood with his hands against the side of the wagon bed and as the moonlight came and went he looked at what he could see without touching. A rug . . . odds and ends of bullets . . . hunks of cloth . . . pans for panning gold . . . an old mothy looking buffalo robe . . . a tin plate to eat off of . . . lots of leaves and dust and dirt over the bottom . . . red dust from last summer showing thru the snow . . . an axe for chopping wood . . . an extra wagon wheel with a broken spoke . . . a bucket of pitch . . . just junk.

Just junk.

Then the Big Fifty caught the moonlight and he lifted it down carefully. He didn't know much about guns and had only the ancient rifle which misfired. He was impressed by the size and weight of the Big Fifty and had to climb up on the wheel to get it all the way down and had to take it out from under the shadow of the two cottonwoods to see it clear in the moonlight and admire its shine, the smoothness of its stock where it was inlaid with silver leaves.

Musta been his huntin gun . . . his treasure . . . take good care of it and should he ever come out of jail I'll give it back all nice and clean . . . I could even leave a note. No, later I'll go down to the fort and I'll find out where he is and then I'll go and tell him I've got his gun.

He propped it by the wagon wheel, then finally laid it down on the ground but remembered that dirt and snow and wetness were not good for guns, so got the mothy buffalo robe and wrapped it up in that and pushed it a little under the wagon.

The leather bag was the next thing that he found. He shook it and wondered what was in it. It gave under the pressure of his fingers like it was filled with dirt and he kept squeezing it and wondering and finally he opened it

194

and stuck one finger inside, but the feel of it didn't tell him much and he was about to throw it down for dirt when he thought it might be gold dust and he wet one finger and stuck inside again and licked the finger which didn't taste like dirt. He took the bag out to the moonlight too and shook out some grains in his hand and squinted at them and then went to the fire and stirred it up to squint again.

By God, I *think* it's gold dust. Ain't it?

He shook out a little more but was careful to see that none fell to the ground and he leaned a little closer to the fire and it glittered some and was kind of yellow.

I think it's gold dust. But whose gold dust. Reckon . . . those men that come and got him . . . did they leave it when they got him? Maybe they even said We'll leave it at the wagon if we catch him. That mighta been and I mighta forgot. Cept it seems like more'n three hunderd. Not that I'm 'quainted with the stuff, but I seen it on the faro tables at the saloon and seemed like . . . think it's more.

Course, the poster was kinda old. Maybe he's worth more. Or maybe it is his. Cause if it is his then I reckon he orter have it so he kin get lawyered with it.

He shook the dust back into the bag being careful to lose none and even set it on the edge of the wagon bed and brushed each grain out of the palm of his hand with the fingers of the other. He tied the bag together again, felt its weight and softness, and slipped it inside his shirt.

Decide that later.

Next he found the velvet box and the touch of it was so familiar and friendly he just rubbed it several times before he took it down and opened it.

Knives, he thought. Wonder if they's what you'd call skinnin knives?

He admired their razor's edge and fine curved blades

and the silver of their hilts and thought here was another treasure. Then he found the doll between them and he went back to the fire with the small doll hanging limp in his hand. It was an ugly thing and he wondered what Rap-aho had kept it for. He turned it in his hands and shook it to see if there was something hidden in it and finally thought it was some Injun thing, maybe even dangerous. He dropped it carefully into the fire, holding it by one whang hand, and kicked some wood chips over it and watched the tongues of flames leap up and burn the husks so quickly but the buckeyes shrivelled slowly and the whang limped first.

He sat back and took the bag of gold dust out of his shirt and played with it.

I reckon I should take it to him so he can get lawyered and they's prob'ly enough so when he gets out of jail he kin start somewheres else . . . maybe buy a little farm. . . .

He pulled his hair some and scratched his neck and thought some more.

He will get out, won't he? Well, sure I think he will. Or . . . I don't know . . . maybe not for murder. I reckon they'll prob'ly   hang   him.

He was surprised he hadn't thought of that before.

My God, I bet they hang him.

The wind blew a little quicker now and he sat back and pulled the Navajo rug over his knees because they were feeling cold. Even his neck felt cold and he pulled some of his hair back and stuffed it into his collar like a scarf. The sky had darkened more with the clouds and the moon was blacked out for a while. But when it came again the wagon seemed to move toward him and the feathers danced like they didn't know the man who put them there was maybe dead.

I think I'll buy a good young horse and a saddle too. And then some saddle bags. I seen some down at Marshall's Store . . . but I wouldn't buy a damn thing from him . . . hell with him. Then I'll get me a good pair of boots, somewhere else, and I'll take a little trip. Scoggins kin look after things while I am gone, cause I'll want to be comin back someday when I'm tired of New Orleans and the iron balconies and the ladies with black hair and plumes of red . . . and then to Santa Fe . . . flowers and red ground and mountains with lots of snow on top . . . and San Francisco and the streets with bricks . . . and to the north . . .

He closed his eyes a moment and drifted back into the world of merchants, rich men, generals and kings. With the bag of gold dust in his hand he dreamed again from the beginning all his dreams. When he came back to earth and the land of poor dirt farmers, it was almost day and a dove was calling.

I kin do it all. I kin even go to the Black Hills and look for Dittany . . . old squaw Dittany . . . what an awful thing to say! I will   go   to   the   Black Hills   honest. Because God has not forgot me and I got the proof right in my hand and I was a good man and did right and said my prayers even when others laughed at me.

But they're gonna hang him.

Another dove answered the first.

He was a old man like me. Only older. Seventy-seventy-five. That's what it said in black. Poor old feller. Even if he was an ornery cuss. Hangin from some tree. Hope it's never where I know. Pass by. Hope they ain't no pain. I mean, they do it quick and he don't kick a lot and hurt his neck. They say it is a terrible way. They say it's hard to watch em too. See em kick. Cause if they is a lot of pain I couldn't never take the money whether it was his or mine. Poor old feller. I never even met him. I was his enemy and he never even knowed it nor got a chance to spit right in my eye.

Course . . . he is so awful old . . . bound to die someday . . . maybe better to have it quick than lay out on some hill like here with a broke leg. . . .

He thought he saw an early hawk above him.

Prob'ly lived his life . . .

The clouds began to break apart.

Not like I lived mine . . . just walked right thru it like it was goin on forever. Never give it a thought till I was so damn old . . . so dumb . . . so poor . . .

The morning star shone bright thru the clouds.

He rubbed his arms to get the chill out of them and slipped one hand up under his sleeve then pushed the sleeve up all the way to warm the arm by the fire because it seemed to be so cold. He looked down at the sagging blue ropes that led from his arms to his fingers. The arm was very thin. Wrinkled. The wrinkles were tanned on top and dirty in their grooves. They were quite even. Like sand seen from a distance that the wind had crossed and ridged. His skin was spotted with brown spots. It also had lots of white marks on it. They were scars. They did not age or tan because the skin was dead, dying with the wound when the blood gushed out of it. The knuckles of his hands were baggy. The skin wound round and round them. They looked like coarse fingerprints of something not quite a man. The bones were very thin too. Beneath the skin they looked yellow and old like chicken feet. The blue ropes were knotted across his hands. They looked as if they had tried to tighten and hold the bones together.

His arms and hands must've looked older'n mine and I

don't see how they kin hang a man as old as that. I just don't see how no human kin throw up a rope and . . .

And I went and turned him in. Just for the money. Might as well be honest. Ain't no one to hear but God and me. I did it for that money. Nothin else. I didn't care all that much about them nesters . . . she was mean. Course I wouldna really have stood and watched him hurt em. But I didn't really mourn em. No. It was for the money. Three hunderd. Just like a Judas is what I done. Course he wasn't no Christ far as that goes. But I still did like a Judas. He never harmed me nor anything nor stole nor lied (course I didn't know him so he could have lied) and I went down and turned him in for that damn three hunderd because I was layin and thinkin bout all them dreams and how it wasn't fair and me playin in the dirt and God . . . but I shouldna have turned him in.

There was a sudden pain going thru his chest and up into his throat where the skin sagged the most. He began to choke all at once for his breath wouldn't come. He heard himself making a whining sound unlike an animal sound and yet less than that of a man. He dropped the bag of gold dust and kicked it from him and scrambled back from it so quick he cracked his head against the tree behind him and he began to rock with his arms around his knees with a motion that was unlike an animal motion and yet less than that of a man.

The sky lightened. Two hawks rode past on the wind. The clouds were tearing apart. But it was still dark down on the ground. Still night.

He began to sweat hard and his tongue became dry. He fell over and crawled toward the stream for water to make the sweat go away and the pain stop and his mouth to feel like his again.

But when he got to the stream and leaned down over, it and reached out to cup the water in his hands . . . there was a man in there. Hidden against the bank of the stream and staring up at him was a man. Frayed eagle feathers quivered in his hat above a strip of red calico. A narrow piece of blue and white pillow ticking was wound round his neck. On his jacket there was fringe, some white men some Injun beaded. His mouth was half open so that the old tooth showed and his face was yellowed and wrinkled and hung with an ugly age and a glittering meanness to the eyes.

He shoved himself back from the stream and heard himself making strange noises and he got to his feet without knowing how and began to run crookedly from the man who'd been hidden there, but who would kill him now.

C-c-can't be no one but Rapaho.

He left behind the gold dust and the gun. The burned up doll he had not recognized. The skinning knives in their velvet case. All he had thought. Dreamed. Hoped. Everything.

The pain was so sharp now that his eyes couldn't see. He stumbled and fell and got up only to stumble and fall again. He thought nothing at all in words.

He felt that he had run a hundred miles thru darkness and he stopped. But when he did he heard the steps of the man behind him. Steady steps. Old steps. Rapaho's steps. He knew the man would have the gun in his hands and when he broke out of the shadows under the skinny trees the man would shoot him. He turned and looked back and tried to tell the man not to shoot him. But when he saw the dark shape and the feathers blowing . . .

It was because he was running backwards that when he hit the bed he didn't know it for what it was. In his mind it was a gunshot. He even saw the flash of fire. Heard the gun boom.

He collapsed down in the snow and rolled over on his back with one hand digging into the snow and he watched the pain flowing out thru his eyes and saw behind it the dark shape coming and the steps.

The mule leaned her head down and nudged him, her mane blowing in the wind like feathers.

But he wouldn't open his eyes to see, for he was sure it was Rapaho.

"D-D-D-Didn't mean to be no Judas," he said.

And he relaxed awhile and the snow seemed warm in his hand.

After a while ke kind of woke again to see two men standing over him, poking at him.

"Sure this's him . . . look there . . . look at that hat with all them feathers . . . and the fringed clothes . . . and all the odds and ends of junk tied on his jacket. . . ."

"Dunno," the other man said, squatting down. "Looks a lot like the other . . . the one that turned him in . . . you know . . . the farmer . . ."

They went away after talking about a shovel.

Hutch lay still, but his head seemed to be walking up and down and jumping sometimes and the pain was back at his throat. It must have been a dream, the men. They came and got him. Or . . . he was hidin . . . yeah, in the stream. . . . But when he tried to raise his arm and wave to them he wasn't dead and he wasn't Rapaho, he saw the fringe on the jacket stand out sharp against the quite light sky, and he saw the silver spoon with its initial, and he saw the rose of satin. The arm that surely was not his in a sleeve he knew to be another man's, fell back to the ground.

"I reckon when you're dyin you see lots of things that

ain't there." He closed his eyes. "But when you're livin you do, too." He tried to move his feet. "One thing I know," he whispered, *"none of this was real."*

Day came on. The sun rose. The wind blew snow over his hands. It drifted over his lashes and now all the lines of his face flattened out like he had been crying and stopped suddenly. There was something about the flat crinkles that was like the face of a boy.

The snow began to fall on the high part of the wrinkles of his face and the high part of the whorls of his knuckles. It left a cold whiteness there that was something like a quilt. Then it fell some more and piled some more, one spot upon the other. It began to be thick. The frozen flowers of the bed were softened and smoked out by the snow. So was he. He grew smokier and smokier as the day went on and the snow kept falling.

The mule, who'd stood off when the other men came by, was back. She pushed the old man with her nose. But he didn't move. She stood by him and waited patiently. But when the snow quit falling and the sun came out and still he didn't move she decided he was like a lot of things that fell down and never moved again and so she left him.

She went down from the hills to the house by the river. The chickens were scratching in the snow. The door was creaking in the wind. There was no reason to be there. There was no one there.

She brayed a time or two but he didn't follow.

She had always wondered why sometimes he ran her to hell and hunt after buffalo and sometimes he went slow, poking along, pointing at flowers and birds. It had never been clear to her that he was two different men in one body. Mules do not understand things like that.

After three days she fell in with a band of mustangs. They never ran up on the high hills above the flat. They winded the hills sometimes. Nickered. The lead mare listening with the others, but always they turned back and never crossed it. Neither did the Injuns, they were on their reservations. Neither did the settlers, there was no trail up there. There was nothing but the grave of the old buffalo hunter, or was it the farmer, that the men from the fort had found dead. An abandoned bed, fallen down. An old bustedy wagon with red paint on its shafts, feathers swinging from it, and HAPY BIRF DAY written on its side. No one ever went up there.

But sometimes when the mustangs grazed at the base of the high hills, they acted skittish, like someone was up there. Especially on nights when the moon was full. And sometimes the grey old mule among them lifted her grizzled jughead, pricked up her ears, for she thought she heard . . .

> *The fox went out on a wintery night,*
> *And he prayed for the moon to give him*
>   *light,*
> *For he'd many a mile to go that night*
> *Before he reached the town-o . . . town-o . . .*
>   *town-o. . . .*